This book belongs to

_____

Children's
POOLBEG

The Long March

A Paperback Original
First published 1990 by
Poolbeg Press Ltd
Knocksedan House,
Swords, Co Dublin, Ireland

Reprinted August 1991

© Michael Mullen 1990

Poolbeg Press receives financial assistance from the Arts
Council/An Chomhairle Ealaíon, Ireland

ISBN 1 85371 109 8

Cover design by Denise Kierans
Set by Richard Parfrey
Printed and bound in Great Britain by
The Guernsey Press Co. Ltd, Guernsey, Channel Islands

The Long March
Michael Mullen

Children's
POOLBEG

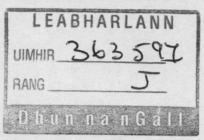
Also by Michael Mullen
in Children's Poolbeg

The Viking Princess
The Little Drummer Boy
The Caravan

For Tom, Des and Conor

Contents

Prologue

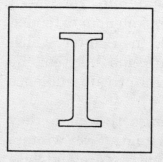t was spring in Spain. Gentle winds blew through the brown central lands, touching the desert with growth. But the plain through which they now passed was brown and arid. The great mountains possessed a hard menacing quality. The metallic blue of the sky cut at their eyes and they had to draw the fine curtains. The ornate carriage moved quickly. It was flanked by royal horsemen and from the standard of the leading rider flew the royal colours. Behind them a cloud of red dust hung in the still air and then fell back onto the dry earth.

Fiach and Emar had rested the previous night at a Spanish inn. They had been served with the finest food, and musicians had played to them through the evening. It was known that they were guests of Philip III. Now they were on the final part of their journey to Madrid. They were excited at the prospect of meeting King Philip. He was a powerful monarch and his kingdom extended across the known world. In a letter which carried both his signature and his seal, he requested them to attend a private audience at the Escorial palace.

As they journeyed across the plain they spoke of their good fortune. Two winters earlier they had marched across Ireland with O'Sullivan Beare. One thousand people had set off from Glengarriff on the last day of the year 1602. Two weeks later only thirty five people reached O'Rourke's castle in Leitrim. The rest had perished on the way or abandoned the march.

It was only now that Emar could recall the long nightmare without distress. The march had left its scars upon her mind and her body. She was sixteen years of age, tall and blonde. Her features were fine and she carried herself like a princess. She was proud of her lineage and she had been received in Spain as one who possessed noble blood.

Her brother Fiach was now fifteen years of

age but looked much older. The march had
hardened him. His face was thoughtful and
he rarely smiled. He had protected his sister
during the long winter march. He had also
dug his mother's grave in a wood close to the
Shannon, while Dermot of Dursey made a
hide boat to ferry the marchers across the
dangerous river.

All Europe had heard of their exploits.
Now the King wished to hear the story from
Fiach, and from Emar, the only woman to
have survived the incredible hardships.

Fiach drew aside the fine curtain and
looked ahead. Out of the plain rose the city of
Madrid. They passed through the city. On
their way through the streets, carriages and
horsemen drew aside to let them pass. They
stopped at the royal stables to change horses;
then they set off again. They drove north-
west for more than twenty miles, excitedly
awaiting a glimpse of the Escorial built for
King Philip II.

The horses approached the great building
of light coloured stone. The road was crowded
with people but they made way for the royal
coach. It passed through the west entrance
which led to the Courtyard of the Kings.
Immediately the carriage halted, two liveried

servants rushed forward to open the door and help Emar and Fiach to the ground. They were directed into the buildings on the right and along several corridors until they arrived at the antechamber of the King. Here they were invited to remain until the King was ready to meet them. They looked in awe at the splendid paintings which covered not only the walls of the room but also the dome above them. The paintings were filled with light and joy. They portrayed delightful feasts of meat, fish, wine and fruits. The woods were bright and fresh; the mountains pastured sheep. The clouds were summer white and the skies were magnificently blue. It was a pleasant, human world without toil or torment.

The doors were thrown open. A servant appeared. "His Majesty will now receive you," he told them.

They passed through the magnificent doors and walked, side by side, to where the King sat on his throne. He indicated that they should sit on two chairs facing him. He had a sharp eye and he looked at them with interest. Beside him, his cartographer had set a map of Ireland.

"I have called you in order to hear the story

of your march at first hand," he said and indicated that Fiach should begin. Quietly, conscious of the importance of the moment, Fiach began the story of The Long March.

1
Fiach and Hugh

The cold was deep, the silence empty in the great wood. The boy blew warmth into his frozen hands. The oak forest was bare, the branches grey. Patches of snow lay in the open spaces. As he looked up through the old and twisted branches of the trees he noticed that the sky was the colour of pewter. He lay on a bed of brittle leaves, his woollen mantle drawn about him. His face was tired but his eyes and ears were alert to every forest movement. He knew that the enemy were sweeping through the forest. They were hunting down fugitives like animals. He must reach the camp of Donal Cam O'Sullivan Beare. Fiach O'Driscoll, the last of his line, felt fear in his stomach.

The images of the last months were

confused and bloody. It was almost a year since the defeat at Kinsale. Since then his life was that of a fugitive. He was afraid to venture out into the open spaces. Though only a boy he had witnessed scenes of carnage which made his blood curdle. During his wanderings he had come upon the corpses of whole families; men, women and children put to the sword by Sir Charles Wilmot. From the edge of the forest he had watched Wilmot's men erect gibbets. Men were placed on army carts and their necks set in the soaped nooses. The carts were drawn away. They dropped, their necks snapped and they looked like straw men. Everywhere there were sudden alarms. The Queen's troops were moving down the peninsula, breaking the final opposition.

During the last months he had visited some strongholds in the area. Everywhere there was anxiety and hunger. He recalled the argument in Con O'Driscoll's dún.

"We are now servants of the queen," one of the young men told the company. "The battle at Kinsale has broken the old powers. It is time to follow the new ways. There is no turning back."

"We should resist to the last drop of our

blood," a hardened veteran replied. "Our ways are not their ways."

"We have waged war for fifteen years. We are beaten and we are divided," Con O'Driscoll argued.

The stronghold had been Fiach's refuge for three days and nights. He had eaten hard oaten bread and drunk milk and he had a rough straw bed upon which to sleep. Now he was alone in the vast oak forest. Somewhere to the north lay the camp of O'Sullivan Beare.

Sleep began to invade his body. He tried to remain awake but he had not slept for twenty-four hours. He was tired and his legs were dull from walking. Despite his best efforts he fell asleep on the forest floor, wedged between the twisted roots of an oak tree.

His fragmented dreams were of quieter days. His mother was singing to him in their castle, close to the sea. Felim, the poet, recited the lists of his ancestors. His line stretched back almost to the beginning of time. Now he was riding across the open fields close to the sea shore. The skies were clear, the meadows speckled with flowers. He saw his sister, Emar, running towards him. He saw his father returning from the hunt, a great antlered deer stretched dead across the saddle. He saw a great ship sailing into Bantry Bay, a wind filling the white sails. And then the Christmas feast in the great hall came into his mind. Oak-logs blazed in the fire place. Ample food was set on the table, flesh and fish and fowl to suit every taste. Wine was poured into silver goblets and his father drank a toast to a prosperous new year.

"Move and you are dead," a rough voice whispered. Fiach opened his eyes and looked into the grim face of a bearded gallowglass.

He felt the cold steel on his throat. He tried to draw a frightened breath. The man who stood above him was huge and his eyes were sharp and dangerous. He wore a shirt of mail over a leather jerkin. His head was protected by a helmet and he carried a large battleaxe and sword. Fiach knew that the man was hungry.

"Who are you and what are you doing in this forest?" the man asked. "You know how dangerous it is?"

"I am of the O'Driscoll sept. Our castle has been razed to the ground by Wilmot's men. I have been separated from my sister and mother. Now I am making my way to Donal Cam's camp. I wish to join his forces as a giolla," Fiach explained.

"Do you carry food in your satchel?" the gallowglass asked.

"Some bread and meat which I obtained some days ago," Fiach said. He had spared the food for many days and had hoped to eat it that evening.

The gallowglass placed his dagger in his belt, took the satchel and drew out the bread and meat. He began to eat it ravenously. The food softened his anger and soon his face relaxed.

"It was a savage war. We were unlucky. At Kinsale we had the English army surrounded but we failed to crush them."

He explained the strategy of the war with his hands. He held them apart. Then he drew them closer slowly. Finally he crushed them together.

"Everything was on our side. The Queen's soldiers were fevered and ill. Yet they broke through our lines and left one thousand of our men dead. The cause is finished. Now I am trapped on this peninsula."

He splayed his fingers and explained to Fiach how they were hemmed in. "I must break through the circle made by Wilmot's men and move to the north. From there I will sail to Scotland. Later I will go to France or Germany. I will hire myself out to some king or prince. If I remain here I will be hunted down and slaughtered."

Fiach was now fully awake and sitting up between the rough roots of the oak tree. "I wish to join the forces of Donal Cam. He fights well and is still holding out," he said.

"Then we will march together. You may carry my axe. I need a giolla. I march with a drawn sword because Wilmot's soldiers are everywhere. They burn the food stores and drive the cattle before them. I must eat to fight and I must fight to eat. Let us move north."

They stood up. Fiach saw that the gallowglass's side had been pierced and a blotch of dried blood stained his jerkin.

"You have been wounded."

"It will heal. It is a shallow wound. My body carries the scars of many battles."

"Does it hurt you?" Fiach asked.

"I do not notice. A soldier must endure pain when he bears arms. It will heal quickly. I am Hugh. What is your name?"

"Fiach."

"Good. Take my axe and let us move towards the north. We will follow the tree shadows. They are vague but they now point north-east," he told him. They began to march through the vast forest.

For a huge man Hugh's foot was light on the forest floor. Periodically he would hold up his arm and Fiach would freeze. Hugh would listen to the deep silence. Once an animal broke a twig and rushed into the thicket. The gallowglass went on the alert, drew his sword, spread his thick legs and waited for some enemy. He searched for the source of the mystery between the trees. Then he relaxed. He beckoned Fiach to follow him. With the haft of the axe across his shoulder Fiach followed the soldier of fortune. He felt protected by the presence of such a man. He trudged forward in his footsteps, knowing that they were going in the general direction of O'Sullivan Beare's camp. If they were to break out of the trap then that was their only chance.

Later they sat down for a rest. It was already getting dark. The cold was deep and searching. Even the gallowglass was shivering.

"I suffer from the cold of hunger. The cold

works from within. I must eat and I must sleep and I must be warm. We will break our march. O'Sullivan Beare can wait. So let us be on the look out for a resting place. It gets dark quickly and we must hasten."

Hugh moved forward more resolutely now. He found a dip in the forest and a cave.

"We will rest here. Now set a fire. Here is some precious tinder. When I return I expect a large blazing fire."

Fiach quickly set about the task. He gathered crisp leaves from the cave and some moss. He formed a cone of the finest twigs about them. Then he flashed the tinder and a starlike spark lodged in the dry moss and started a fire. Soon the flames were licking through light branches. He ran in search of more fuel, joyful in his new task.

It was dark when Hugh returned. He carried a young suckling pig across his shoulder.

"We will eat as well as Wilmot tonight," he said. His humour had improved greatly. He drew great branches from the forest and set them on the fire. When the heart of the fire was a steady glow, he set the suckling pig on a spit. Then, sitting in the mouth of the cave and out of the cold, they looked at their supper cooking. Soon their nostrils were filled with the aroma of roasting meat.

"It will put heart into us for tomorrow," Hugh remarked as he removed the spit. He plunged it into the ground and taking his knife, carved delicious slices from the back of the roast pig. He handed Fiach the first slice. The boy took it in his hands and threw it about from hand to hand until it was cool. Then he ate the meat. It was like honey on his tongue. Hugh ate ravenously, eating four slices for every one that Fiach ate. "I have enough," Fiach said finally.

"I never have enough. I am always hungry. I'm hungry before battle and I'm hungry after battle." But finally Hugh too was satisfied.

"We will have a breakfast out of the pig's feet in the morning. It will start us on our way." Hugh put his arms about his stomach and laced his fingers as if to protect his food. "Now tell me your story and I shall tell you mine," he said in a relaxed mood.

Sitting at his ease before the fire, which had now collapsed into a warm glow, Fiach told Hugh his story. Their castle stood above the sea, commanding a view of great beauty. After the defeat of Kinsale his father had returned to the fortress and withstood several attacks by regiments sent against him. But gradually the forces of Wilmot began to wear him down. They broke into the paddock and stole a prey of cattle, knowing that the defenders would grow hungry and weak within the walls. And finally a culverin had been drawn across the mountain and set on a flat crag above the castle. Day after day it pounded on the walls, bringing down the masonry. When the outer ramparts had been breached, the soldiers poured through. A dreadful battle followed in the inner bailey. Most of the starving defenders were slaughtered and those who remained, including his father, were hanged in front of women and children.

"It was a horrible sight. I can never clear the memory from my mind. It comes back to me in sleep," he told Hugh.

"Death is a terrible thing," Hugh said solemnly. "But continue your story."

"I escaped from the burning castle. I looked back and watched the weeping women remove the dead bodies from the gallows. I have not heard news of my mother or sister since. I took refuge in woods. That was some three weeks ago. I only ventured out from the shelter of the forest to beg for bread. I have knocked at the doors of dúns where I was once welcome only to be turned away."

Hugh sighed. "The old ways of friendship are disappearing. I know. I have soldiered in Ireland for fifteen years. I have enjoyed the hospitality and friendship. But now men must change to the English ways. They must bow to Queen Elizabeth and receive new titles. But let us sleep and regain our lost strength."

They entered the cave which was partly lit by the glow from the fire. They lay on the comfort of the dry heather and leaves.

"Prod me if I snore," Hugh said before he drew his large mantle about him. "I have kept a regiment of soldiers awake with the same snoring."

With that he lay on his back. His face fell into repose. Beside him lay his sword.

Fiach looked at the red glow of the fire for a moment. It was like a warm heart in the menacing darkness. Then, happy in his good fortune at meeting Hugh, he lay back on the ground and drew his woollen cloak about him. Hugh began to snore to a deep rhythm. He drew in great draughts of air, then snorted them out like an angry bull. But Fiach had no wish to wake him. Soon he was overcome by the warmth and comfort of the cave and fell into a deep sleep.

Outside it began to snow. The large flakes fell slowly over the bare forest, filling hollows and ruts. But even at night-time horsemen passed through the forest. They never rested. They drove away the preys of cattle and burned corn stores. Those not defeated in open battle would be broken by starvation and famine.

Fiach was the first to awaken. The winter light, whitened on the snow, filled the cave. Hugh had stopped snoring. His face was in deep repose, no longer bitter with hunger. It carried the scars of many battles but now had the gentleness of a child.

Fiach looked out at the snow which lay softly on the open hollow. Only a charred stump jutting up out of the snow marked the position of the night fire. He let Hugh sleep. He drew up his knees and held them with his hands. He reflected on the last few terrible weeks and he wondered if they would ever reach the camp of O'Sullivan Beare.

Hugh opened one eye and then another. He stared at the roof of the cave for a moment and took stock of his position. He then rubbed the sleep out of his eyes and began to draw the sharp morning air into his lungs.

"You slept well?" he asked Fiach, still lying flat upon his back.

"Yes. Very well. It is the best night of sleep I had in a very long time."

"Good. My strength returns when I sleep well. And did I snore?"

"Yes. But I quickly fell asleep and did not hear."

"Good. Then we are now prepared to meet the dangers of the day." And with that Hugh sat up. His whole character had changed. His voice was lighter and his eyes sparkled brightly.

"Let us eat," he ordered and he dismembered the remains of the suckling pig which they began to eat slowly.

"What wouldn't I give for a good draft of beer to wash my food down," Hugh remarked as he chewed on the ribs and the bones. "Today we will continue northeast and by my reckoning we should eventually reach the camp of O'Sullivan Beare. Our hope lies with him. He is the best leader one could have, courageous and alert."

When the sun was well into its first quarter, they prepared to move out of the hollow in which they had taken refuge. Hugh carried his great sword and Fiach, now his giolla, carried his double-edged axe, a heavy and formidable weapon.

"Stay close to me," said Hugh. "If you grow weary, tell me and we shall rest. One has to march rapidly. It is necessary if one is to make progress. You must continue on even if your legs ache. And remember, keep your eyes wide open for danger and your ears alert for the least sound."

With that advice Hugh moved forward up the hollow followed by Fiach, the heavy axe on his shoulder.

They passed through the forest, the great oak trunks standing about them, firm and old and certain. The trees afforded them protection against the advance of horse soldiers. But they knew that hidden eyes would be watching them. The countryside was filled with spies ready to hasten to the enemy camp with information which was worth a silver piece or a bowl of food.

But then they walked into the trap. They had moved from the protection of the forests and taken a wide exposed path which led steeply down from the mountain flank. When they were half way down the incline they heard the neigh of horses. They looked behind them. From higher up in the forest two riders emerged, their swords drawn, urging their horses forward. They charged towards the gallowglass and the boy, gathering speed on the slope as they moved.

Fiach shook with fear. For a moment he wished to rush to the shelter of the forest but Hugh grasped his cloak. "Behind me," he ordered. Hugh faced the enemy, his sword grasped in both hands and pointing towards the ground. He nerved himself for the onslaught. From behind his back, Fiach watched the menacing riders rush forward. As they charged down upon them in the exposed place, Hugh made no move. It was only when the riders were twenty feet from where he stood in the snow that he sprang into action. Letting out a great cry, which threw the horses into confusion, he rushed forward, catching the enemies off balance. Before they had time to raise their swords to bring them down upon him, Hugh had stepped to one side and cut through the guard of the soldier on the right, knocking his sword from him and wounding him in the side. As the second soldier tried to charge past them, Hugh whipped out his dagger and with a quick flick, threw it. It lodged between the

shoulders of the confused enemy. He fell
forwards on his horse and continued to ride
down through empty space. Soon both of
them disappeared across the brow of a hill.
The whole action had happened in a few
seconds. When Fiach finally drew himself to
his feet, Hugh was quietly wiping the blood
from his sword on to the snow.

"I thought that they would kill us," he said
to Hugh.

"They did not count on my experience and
training," the other man replied. "If I had fled
they would have chased me down like an
animal. They were fools. They gave me time
to prepare myself. Now I must go and recover
my dagger."

"But they are miles away by now," Fiach
told him.

"We shall see," answered Hugh.

Gallowglass and boy continued to trudge
forward through the snow. As they came over
the brow of the hill, they saw one horse
standing riderless in the snow. Further on lay
the soldier in the soft snow. The dagger was
still embedded in his back.

Hugh drew it out and wiped it in the snow.
Then he replaced it in his belt. He searched
the body for money, found some coins and

placed them in his small sporran. He drew off the soldier's boots and handed them to Fiach.

"Someone at the camp of O'Sullivan Beare will have better use for these," Hugh said without feeling. "And he has made our journey shorter. Let us take the horse." He jumped into the saddle, drew Fiach up behind him and set off.

Much later in the day they saw a peasant gathering wood at the edge of the forest. He drew himself up in terror when he saw them approach. He fell on his knees and began to cry out. "Spare me. I wish only to gather some dry branches to keep my family warm. We are without food or fuel."

Hugh looked at the miserable wretch, badly clothed and with a torn ear cap on his head. "Direct us to the camp of O'Sullivan Beare," he ordered sternly.

"It's three miles to the north, past the hills with the chapel ruins," the peasant said, pointing to a distant hill. "But I fear you will find no comfort there. It is said that Wilmot has robbed O'Sullivan of his prey of cattle and the camp goes hungry."

Hugh took the coins he had recently removed from the dead soldiers pocket and threw them on the snow. "Buy what you can for your family, if money still has any value."

While the peasant scraped in the snow for the coins Hugh turned the horse in the direction of the hill and kneed him forward. The light was now beginning to fail. Soon he could see the black outlines of the ruins on the hill. When they reached the crest of the hill and looked at the far valley they saw the camp of O'Sullivan Beare. Smoke ascended from the fires about which people stood. It was getting cold and a wind blew across the hill, with a lonely moan.

They moved down towards the camp.

2
Emar and Her Mother

Sir Charles Wilmot drank the mulled wine. Captured from a Spanish ship in Bantry bay, it had been intended for his enemies. He sat in the inn before a blazing fire. The room was low and comfortable. Great oak-beams, rough-hewn, carried the black ceiling. Pewter tankards hung from wooden pegs and reflected the roaring flames. On a massive oak table lay the remnants of a great dinner. Both he and his captains had supped well on roast and venison.

Wilmot was pleased. The great campaign was drawing to a close. There were a few pockets of resistance to mop up. Then it would be finished. It had lasted too long. Many of the English soldiers lay exhausted and ill in Cork. But a thousand new recruits had been gathered to form an army.

Now thirty-two, Sir Charles Wilmot possessed a sharp intelligent face. His mind was alert to all that was happening in the Beare peninsula, that rough finger of land, with its backbone of central hills, which stretched out into the Atlantic Ocean. He had assisted Sir George Carew at the the siege of Dunboy castle. When the castle was taken after much savage fighting, fifty-eight survivors were hanged. The stronghold of O'Sullivan Beare was now a ruin. O'Sullivan Beare was a fugitive. He was hemmed in and soon would be destroyed.

Wilmot awaited the arrival of Lord Barry and Sir George Thornton. As he drank his red wine with his captains, they recalled the campaigns they had fought. They remembered the dangers and the wounds. Each could show some scar received during the battles. As they grew merry, they began to sing in harmony Ben Jonson's "Drink to me only with thine eyes." The inn was filled with their resonant voices.

Outside the snow was beginning to fall. The soldiers who stood on guard duty about the inn cursed their ill fortune as they listened to the merriment within.

"Not a decent morsel of meat passed my lips this week and this the season of Christmas," an old soldier complained.

"The smell of the roasting meat within makes me hungry. I wish I were with my wife and child in Cork. It's no time for a Christian to be abroad," his friend answered.

"They have no regard for this season, only a desire for the death of the enemy. While they feast they know that men perish from famine in the forests."

"I wish I were within." One soldier left his post and went to the window. He gazed at the great fire and table laden with food. His teeth became wet with saliva and he felt cold and hungry. He watched the captains toast each other.

"How goes it within, George?" asked his comrade when he returned.

"They drink the red wine from their tankards and sing sweet songs of women. I wonder where is our friend Peter."

They heard soft footsteps in the snow. "Who goes there?" they asked, grasping their swords.

"Who do you think? Peter, and I bring you warm drink." He carried a large wooden mug filled with raw whiskey. "Drink. It will keep our enemy the cold at bay."

They passed the mug between them. The raw liquor warmed their stomachs.

Suddenly horse soldiers appeared out of the darkness and rode down the village streets. The sentries grasped their swords and waited for the troop to approach.

"Who goes there, friend or enemy? "

"Friends, you fools! Is Sir Charles Wilmot within?" a haughty voice asked.

"He is indeed."

"Then announce that Lord Barry and Sir George Thornton have arrived."

One of the soldiers knocked at the door. It was opened by a servant woman.

"Tell the company that Lord Berry and Sir George Thornbush have arrived," the soldier said drunkenly.

"Lord *Barry* and Sir George *Thornton*, you fool!" the rider corrected him.

"Are you drunk man?" Lord Barry asked as he brushed past the sentry.

"No my Lord. Not a drop of liquor has passed my lips this week. My mind is ravelled for want of food."

"Churl," said Barry and brought the flat blade of his sword down on the soldier's head.

He cried out in agony and fell to his knees. He was holding his head in pain when his friends came to lift him into a standing position.

"I do not know why I am a soldier," he told his friend.

"And neither do I. And our good liquor spilt on the snow."

They took up their posts and resumed guard.

For Lord Barry and Sir George Thornton another keg of wine was opened. The two gentlemen drew their daggers and carved slices of beef and venison. They then stood before the fire and warmed themselves. They took the tankards of wine offered by the servants and drank the health of Queen Elizabeth.

Outside the whole army had assembled. About the dark village men started to light fires against the cold. As the men mingled, they began to swap stories with each other. They had been tested in bloody campaigns and felt little compassion for their enemies. In satchels they carried their rations. They ate roughly and ravenously. Some played dice while others sharpened their swords and axes. Some cleaned their guns by the blazing light of the fire.

"O'Sullivan Beare stands no chance against such an army," Peter, the sentry, remarked. "By spring the wars will be over."

The revelry within the tavern stopped. Now the sentries could hear the voices of soldiers talking and the crackle of burning wood.

"The captains have fallen silent," Peter's friend said. "Go and peep in at the window and see what passes between them."

Peter crept to the window and peered inside. The captains stood about a map, involved in heated discussions. They were planning the final campaign.

"I will not move until I am certain of O'Sullivan's position," Sir George Wilmot said. "I will not expose my men to the hazards of the weather. If possible we will avoid direct battle. If we cut off his supplies then O'Sullivan will perish or he will sue for clemency."

"Not O'Sullivan Beare. He is proud and haughty. The others you can starve into submission but not this man," an officer said.

"Then we will watch him weaken and we'll harass him. A man without food in his stomach has no stomach for battle. My spies have gone in search of his camp. We will retire to bed and wait. Good night, gentlemen." Wilmot's voice was commanding and the others fell silent. One by one they left the inn and sought rough billets in the village. The three commanders slept in comfortable beds.

The sentries were relieved after midnight. Their hands and feet were cold so they sat by the campfire. They were soon warmed by the rough whiskey and they munched on rye bread.

The two women moved through the forest, wearing heavy shawls drawn about their shoulders. They were exhausted with fatigue. The younger woman encouraged the older to continue walking.

"If we rest now, the wind will chill our bodies and we shall die. We must reach the comfort of a house," the girlish voice argued.

"I am tired. We have travelled all day without food and I feel that I have little strength remaining in me. I must sit for a moment and draw my breath," said the older woman. "I wish we were at home in peace. These wars have destroyed all the decencies of life."

"There is no home to go to and we cannot turn back having come so far. Tomorrow we shall reach O'Sullivan's camp," said the girl.

They listened to the wolves howl in the wood. The cries were getting louder and they felt the presence of the ferocious animals close at hand.

The snow was falling on the high hills and on the oak forest. They wiped the flakes from their eyes and peered into the darkness. They feared they would get lost or move only in circles, forever returning to the same position like some damned spirit.

But the older woman did find some strength in her body. Facing into the snow, she pushed forward. Through the forest the two women saw the camp fires burn. The warm cones of light drew them as the moth is drawn to the flame. They moved nearer and listened to the sound of men talking by the camp fire.

"It is Wilmot's army," the younger woman said. "We will receive no welcome there. Let us return to the safety of the forest."

"Surely they would not refuse us bread at this sacred season," said the older woman.

"No season is sacred to soldiers. They would cut us down without a thought."

"These are evil times. I remember Christmas-time at the castle when we drew in the great oak logs and set them to burn. And how your father greeted the poor and welcomed them to his table. We had the best of meat and the best of drink. It seems so long ago. It seems like a dream," the older woman said.

"Do not talk. It weakens your strength. We must not give up now."

The two women fell silent and pushed forward through the snow. It was a long exhausting night. But as morning broke and the first light pierced the forest, they felt some small hope in their hearts. They had followed the mountain path and now they could see the lowlands where the snows had not yet fallen. The smell of turf smoke came to them and they heard the lowing of cattle. They knew that they were approaching the camp of O'Sullivan Beare. They had survived a long journey.

At daybreak the spies arrived at Wilmot's camp. They were men of low cunning who traded their knowledge for food. They were brought directly into Wilmot's presence despite their filth and weariness.

"Where is O'Sullivan's camp?" he asked them.

"Three hours march from here," one spy answered.

"And the setting?"

"Low ground and in a hollow place. You can approach it through the forest. "

"And how many armed men serve O'Sullivan Beare?"

"Half as many as are camped here."

"And what of their cattle and sheep?"

"Twice as many sheep as cattle. And half as many garrans as horses."

"And the condition of the army?"

"Many have deserted O'Sullivan Beare and set off to the north but he still has a goodly number."

"Three hours march from here?"

"Three hours march, perhaps four, for the snow is heavy in parts."

"Very well. You will receive food and shelter. Take this note to the quarter master," Wilmot said, taking his quill and writing some numbers on a piece of paper. "But be at hand...I may need you for a further mission."

The leader took the note and with the others left the room.

"Open the door and let out the stench," Wilmot ordered his servant.

He poured some wine and drinking from the tankard, examined the map which stood before him. It had been done in some detail and he knew the exact location of O'Sullivan Beare's camp. He must now plot his strategy.

He had no desire to engage in open combat. His best ally was starvation and hunger. Whenever he came upon the corn supplies of the enemy, he had burned them. He planned to cut off O'Sullivan Beare's food supply. Perhaps he could set up a diversion and draw away O'Sullivan's army. Then his own troops would descend upon the cattle, sheep and garrans. Wilmot decided to remain another night in the village and let his men rest. They were well supplied with food and drink and that night they toasted Wilmot with red Spanish wine.

Next morning, flanked by the army of Lord Barry, Wilmot set out.

Donal Cam O'Sullivan Beare possessed a fine sharp face and piercing eyes. His aquiline nose added to the severity of his features. He had watched his fortunes fail during the summer. As the leaves fell in the forests he knew that the winds were blowing away his protection. He had moved quickly across the Beare peninsula, attacking the enemy positions, burning their castles and then disappearing as quickly as he appeared. He hoped that more Spanish help might arrive. It would spark off another rebellion and the scattered remnants would flock to his flag. But winter had come. His hopes faded. His men were weary and several bands of soldiers had deserted the peninsula and headed north towards Connacht and Ulster.

O'Sullivan's position was growing desperate. Now some four hundred able bodied men remained together with some six hundred camp followers who depended upon him for their safety. Near the camp some soldiers guarded his food supply. The thin cattle and sheep, whittled of substance, might nourish his camp during the winter but all over Munster starvation was rife and he knew that people were dying like flies.

When O'Sullivan looked towards the forest he was surprised to see horse-soldiers emerge into the open and form battle lines. He ordered his men into their positions and soon they were locked in deadly combat. Meanwhile, more troops who had lain hidden in the forest emerged and descended towards the cattle and sheep pens. Before O'Sullivan could regroup his men the cattle and sheep were already fleeing before the enemy. He ordered his men to follow them but it was too late to cut them off. O'Sullivan Beare returned to his camp. His face had an expression of despair. He knew that the meagre rations would sustain his followers only for some two days. Then, like others all over Munster, they would starve. He must make a rapid decision.

3
O'Sullivan's Plan

ilmot's soldiers pressed the cattle, sheep and horses rapidly through the snow. They charged along the animals' flanks, beating them heavily with their swords. The animals were exhausted. But Wilmot was anxious to push forward with his prize. Riders now carried lanterns to direct them through the darkness. Finally they reached the village. They drove the cattle into the main street and penned them in. A heavy guard was mounted about them. Wilmot ordered several animals to be slaughtered to feed his men.

"And break out more barrels of wine. The men have fought bravely and deserve to toast their victory," Wilmot told his lieutenants. That night Peter and his friend chewed on mutton and beef. They watched the cuts of meat braise over the fire, turning slowly and browning. Great gobs of fat fell into the fire and fuelled it.

"While Munster starves we'll sup like kings," they toasted each other.

Wilmot was flushed with victory. His captains and companions gathered about the table and drank freely. The excitement of the encounter was still in their blood.

"The great O'Sullivan Beare fell for the oldest and simplest ruse in the game of war. His attention was diverted from the main attack of the army," one of the captains laughed.

"He fought well. Six hours is a long time in the field and his men were exhausted. One must admire such courage," Wilmot admitted.

"And shall we press our advantage?" asked another of the captains.

"It is already being pressed for us. I will not commit my army again to the field. Now I shall let General December and General January do my work for me," said Wilmot. "We have sufficient food to carry us through the winter. By then the rebels will be starved into submission. The war in Munster is drawing to a close and the chieftains are almost beaten. The Queen's law will now run in this rebellious land. And so we will winter in some walled and comfortable town. The battles are now over. Let's drink a toast to victory."

"Victory!" they called solemnly and held their wine cups high. They were fighting men who had acquitted themselves well during the campaign.

"And what will O'Sullivan Beare do now? To whom shall he turn?" a captain asked.

"At this moment he is considering his position. It was difficult—now it is impossible. Yet he will not submit to our law. I believe that he will break out of the peninsula and travel north," said Wilmot.

"Should we not follow him and wear him down?"

"The weather and the terrain will do that. Besides, I have a further plan which I will put into operation as soon as he makes his move. For the moment let us sit in the warmth of this comfortable inn and let the hard winter play upon a weakened enemy. It will hound him like a pack of ravening wolves. I have men posted in the woods above his camp. They will carry dispatches to us at intervals."

"To the health of Sir Charles Wilmot," the captains toasted. He smiled at the company and drank from his silver cup.

Donal Cam O'Sullivan Beare rested before one of the camp-fires. Sitting on a great log he looked into the flames. He felt weary. The fighting had taken its toll of his mind. If he remained in the Beare peninsula he and his troops would perish. There was only one course of action. He must move rapidly to the north and reform there. He could join forces with O'Neill and O'Donnell. The old cause was not yet dead.

The year was drawing to a close. It had been an unlucky year, a calendar of failures. O'Sullivan's castle lay in ruins, his followers had been slaughtered, help had not arrived from Spain and he was pitted against a callous and brilliant enemy. Everywhere the old cause lay in ruins. Even his former friends were submitting to the English Queen and the English system.

O'Sullivan left the fire and walked through the camp. There women tended the soldiers' wounds. Children cried because of the cold. Others called for food, of which very little now remained. He reckoned that the oatmeal and bread would feed them for two days at most; then they would have to live off the land. He must protect people who could claim relationship with him through blood or marriage. It was a firm and old bond which he must honour.

It would be a long march. There would be casualties and O'Sullivan Beare knew that graves would mark his journey towards Ulster. He called aside his uncle. Dermot O'Sullivan was now seventy years of age. His body had been toughened by the wars. His grey beard and rutted face marked the passage of hard times.

"I did not dare interrupt your thoughts as you sat beside the fire," his uncle told Donal Cam. "But I knew that you were making some final decision."

"Decisions are difficult, Dermot. There is no easy way out of the position in which we now find ourselves. If we remain we will be hunted like animals. I am too proud to submit to Mountjoy, Carew or Wilmot. What would you do in my situation?"

Dermot O'Sullivan took a branch and threw it onto the blazing fire. He reflected for some time. "The cause has collapsed. We can never hope to regain our power. My heart

would like to believe that we stand some
chance of bringing our old friends together in
a last campaign. But my reason tells me that
our campaigns are over. I fight now only to
stay alive. We must leave this place. But no
ship sails towards Spain."

"Then we move towards the north," said
his nephew.

"It is a desperate measure in the depths of
winter. We must pass across bleak mountains
and ford rivers. Everywhere we will
encounter dangers and enemies. For I can
assure you that they will prey upon us. And
Wilmot would prize your head at this
moment."

"We will move quickly and soon. We will
move out on the last day of the year."

"And may all the ill fortune which has
dogged us be left behind with the old year,"
the old man added earnestly.

"But you know the slim chance we have.
Even O'Neill's soldiers were attacked and
robbed on their return journey. Now the
condition of the country is more desperate.
When men are hungry they have no
allegiance. We march at a bad time of year
and a bad time in history. But I abide by your
decision. It is the only one possible."

"Will the others agree?" the younger man asked.

"I will talk to them. I believe they will."

"Then let us sleep. I do not think that we shall be harassed this night. But I know that eyes from the forest will watch our blazing fires."

After he had set sentries about the camp O'Sullivan went to his tent, drew his great mantle about him and fell asleep. Years in the field had trained him to sleep and gather his energies.

Next morning news spread quickly among those in the camp. They were to break out of the peninsula and march north. Many of the women cursed O'Sullivan for his decision. They had no wish to leave the hills and glens with which they were familiar. They persuaded their men to leave the security of the camp and journey down into the peninsula. O'Sullivan Beare watched them go with a cold stoical eye.

Quietly the rest prepared for the departure. Men sharpened their swords and javelins; others feathered their arrows, softened the bow gut, tested their guns. They were aware of the dangers ahead but Spanish gold would hold their allegiance.

For Emar and her mother the camp offered little solace. From the moment of their arrival they felt that they were a burden upon the others. Now with the food supply cut off they were feeling hungry.

"I shall go and beg some food from O'Sullivan Beare," Emar told her mother.

"We were never beggars."

" We are now!" her daughter replied.

"Then we have fallen on hard times, my daughter."

"Yes Mother," and with that Emar went over to O'Sullivan Beare's tent. He stood with his men discussing tactics. She stood some distance from them.

"Well, woman? Why do you tarry? Are you not preparing to move out with the others?" asked O'Sullivan.

"I have no food and neither has my mother. We have recently arrived at the camp and hope for protection and succour."

He recognised her. "You are Tadhg O'Driscoll's daughter. How you have grown." He went into his tent and brought her a large rough cake and a tankard of wine. "Carry that to your mother. It will cheer her."

Emar returned to her mother. She ate the

rough bread delicately. It was sweet in her mouth. Then she sipped the wine. It reminded her of the great feasts at their castle many years ago.

"It will make me drunk, daughter," she said.

"No it will warm your body and you need warmth for the journey ahead."

"We go without the protection of a man. I feel that our strength will not bear up to the strenuous demands of the march," the older woman said.

Emar and her mother fell silent and ate their food. They did not notice the two figures who stood out, black against white, as they moved down the snow. It was only when they were at the edge of the camp that Emar recognised her brother, Fiach. He was with a gallowglass of immense stature.

"Mother, mother," Emar called, pulling at her mother's shoulder. "Our prayers have been answered. Fiach is here."

"Where? Where?" the old woman asked as she looked about her. Then she recognised her son. Emar called to Fiach. He jumped from the horse and rushed towards her. They clasped each other without speaking.

"There is so much I have to tell you," he

said.

"We thought that you were dead."

"I escaped into the forests and took my chances there."

Great tears rolled from his mother's eyes. She wrapped her mantle about him.

While they talked, Hugh the Gallowglass dismounted. Men whispered amongst themselves. Hugh's feats in battle were known to all. His body carried scars from all the battles he had been through. Men feared his presence both in battle and in the camp.

Hugh walked towards Fiach and his mother. She looked in wonder at the gallowglass.

"My son tells me that you saved his life. For that I thank you."

"He is a brave lad. He will march with me and carry my sword and tend my horse," said Hugh.

"Then he will have to march far towards the north."

"Good. I am tired of Munster. We have failed here. I will hire myself to some chieftain in Ulster or perhaps in Scotland. And when do we march?" Hugh asked.

"On the dawn of the last day of the year," Emar replied.

"Then we must prepare," Hugh said, "for you will march under my protection."

"The saints are on our side," said Fiach's mother.

"We have brought you a gift," Fiach said to his mother. "Look!" He took the soldiers' boots from the saddle. "Try them on. They are warm and your sandals are thin."

She tried the boots but they were too large.

"Bind your feet with linen strips," Fiach told her. "They will save you against the cold."

"I must see how conditions are," Hugh said, as he left them.

Purposefully he strode through the camp. He was not pleased by what he saw. There were too many camp followers who would hinder the progress of the army.

He approached the tent of O'Sullivan Beare. "I am Hugh the Gallowglass," he saluted.

"Your reputation goes before you," O'Sullivan Beare replied.

"I come to offer my services. I believe that you pay well in gold coin. For triple pay I shall march in the most dangerous position."

"Do you deserve triple pay?"

"Ask my enemies!" Hugh replied.

O'Sullivan Beare fetched the money. and counted it into the gallowglass's large palm.

Then Hugh went among the camp followers. He knew that there were deserters ready to leave the camp at nightfall. He let it be known that he would purchase excess baggage for Spanish gold. Secretly they came to him and parted with bread and mantles and shoes in return for the gold.

He spread out what he had purchased before Fiach, Emar and their mother. "We have sufficient food for four days in this saddle bag. The horse needs oats and I have purchased enough for him. After that we will have to live off the land. Now wrap yourselves in mantles and sleep as well as you can. You will need all your strength."

Darkness came quickly. In the hills and on the mountain flanks the snow was falling though not yet in the valley in which they camped. And as darkness fell, people slipped out of the camp and moved up towards the forest. Then the camp fell still. A few men sat humped above the fires, their minds numb and blank. A few threw dice. But most gathered themselves in their mantles, lay close to the fires and slept. As the fires died the sentries deserted their posts, drew close

and soon they too fell into sleep. From the
forests the spies watched.

4
The March Begins

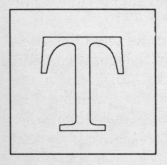he dawn broke wet and grey. It was the last day of the year 1602. The camp began to stir. Men blew frosted breath into their hands to warm them. They beat their arms about their bodies to stir the blood. They stamped their feet on the iron earth. The women gathered the bedclothes, drawing them into bundles and strapping them on to the baggage animals. Grooms and giollas were preparing their masters' arms and tackling horses. The horsemen carried shirts of mail and armour. The gallowglasses donned their leather jerkins and their head pieces.

The soldiers always followed the same morning ritual. They had their food carried to them by the giollas and, having eaten, they

took their weapons, tested them and belted
on their swords. Then they fell into the order
of march. The army was efficient, battle
tested and could endure great hardship. It
knew how to deal with the enemy and would
show no mercy.

Within an hour of dawn the tents had been
folded and strapped to the baggage animals.
The army was in position; horsemen in the
rear and in front of them foot soldiers. The
civilians were in the centre and at the head of
the army stood two hundred kerns and
gallowglasses.

Before he joined the front rank, Hugh gave
Fiach careful directions. "You must keep the
pace. Put tiredness at the back of your mind
and force yourself forward. I have been on
such marches before. If you weaken, you will
be left to die of cold or by the sword of the
enemy."

"My mother grows weak," cried Emar.

"She may ride on horseback later but at
present she marches with the rest of us."
Hugh's voice was without compassion.

"He is cruel," Emar said.

"He understands the ways of war," her
mother told her. "We must follow his orders.
Our safety now lies with him."

Hugh moved to the head of the long column. His great size was impressive. He would force the march forward. He took his place in the front line, raised his hand, then drew it down in a signal and stepped forward. The long march had begun.

The rough road lay close to the sea. To the south lay the wide bay of Bantry from where many ships had sailed to Spain with their cargoes of exiles. The great bay was now empty. To the north they still had the shelter of the hills. But when they reached the mouth of Coomhola river they began to ascend into the mountains. They had their last view of the great bay. But the pace did not slacken and there was little time for tears. O'Sullivan had already decided that they should march by Carriganass castle. It was the longest route to Gougane Barra but the safest. The winds gathered force and carried the sharp edge of winter. They bent their heads and pushed forward. People and horses stumbled. They were drawn roughly into line and the march continued. They ate as they marched. Close to Douce mountain the first casualty occurred. An old woman missed her step and rolled screaming down a sharp decline, her body torn by rough stones. The screaming stopped. The body continued to gather pace until it fell limply into the bed of a stream.

The column was startled by the thin scream. They would have halted but a horse soldier urged them forward. "Keep moving. We have no time for funeral rites. The woman is dead. There is nothing we can do."

Dumbly they moved forward. The winds now were hard and harsh, crying like old women wailing. People were breathing hard as they pushed upward into the mountains. Finally they reached the pass of Keamaneigh. On one side stood a harsh crag of rock, on the other a sharp slope. They kept their eyes peeled as they passed through the awesome place. Here an enemy could take up position and hurl spears at them. But they passed through in safety and began to descend towards Gougane Barra. Finally they reached the lake in the small glen, with its ancient ruins. Rough mountains stood about it, sinister and dark and on the flanks of the mountains great oak forests grew. The marchers had only time to draw their breath there, for night would soon be upon them and they must reach the ruined church of Eachros some miles away.

"This old man needs to rest. If he continues

to march he will surely die," a daughter complained to one of the soldiers.

"Leave him to die here. It is a sacred place," the soldier answered roughly.

"I'll die here," the old man said. "You must move on without me. I am a burden to you."

His daughter stayed at the side of the road with her father, comforting him with her soft voice.

"Is there no pity?" Emar asked as she passed the old man and the woman.

"No," Fiach replied. "We must continue while the light holds in the sky."

They had walked twenty miles over rough terrain but they still had several miles to go before night. The pace quickened. Hugh called out that they would rest within the hour. The great column fell silent. Only the crunch of feet could be heard and the sound of the sad wind. Now the snow began to fall again. It covered them with soft flakes. They bent into the wind and continued onward.

Finally the gable of the ancient church loomed in the dusk. The marchers gathered about it and felt protected. Wearily they sat down and began to eat the rough bread they had carried with them. Limbs ached and people wished to sleep. They knew that at dawn they would be marching again. They must travel during the short light.

The giollas set up O'Sullivan Beare's tent. Before he retired he walked among his people who saw that his face was drawn and he talked very little. O'Sullivan's men told him that three people had died on the march and several had turned back.

"And so our band grows smaller. Have any of the soldiers deserted?"

"No," answered a soldier.

"Good. Our fighting force has been maintained. Soon I expect our first attack. Set a guard. I shall now retire to my tent." O'Sullivan moved away.

Meanwhile, close to the wall, Hugh had skilfully set up an awning for the two women.

"Now get as much sleep as you can. Tomorrow we will march even further," he told Emar and her mother.

They felt secure beneath the awning. They drew their mantles about them and soon they were asleep.

"The men must sleep in the open," Hugh told Fiach. "Soon your body grows accustomed to the harsh weather. And always sleep with an ear cocked. I know when an animal passes through the forest or when an enemy approaches."

"Are you pleased with the march so far?" Fiach asked.

"We move as rapidly as we can with baggage and people. But soon the old and the weak will fall and die on the side of the road. And all the battles lie ahead of us. I know some of the country through which we will pass. Were we victors they would run to us. But they know that we have been beaten. They will harry us like wolves. I should not tell you of these things. You did well today. Now you too must sleep and so must I."

Hugh and Fiach drew their rough cloaks about them and lay against the old walls of Eachros church. Soon they were asleep. Some snow fell on the graveyard and covered them but they were sound asleep and they did not notice.

The spies shook themselves awake. It was late. They had slept deep in the forest in a bothy which they had discovered. In a hollow they had built a fire and warmed their cold meat. They drank the wine they carried and then retired to the bothy.

Now they ate their breakfast of bread and butter, mounted their horses and set out for their vantage points. As they peered from the forest down towards the camp they were amazed. It no longer existed. Only the charred remains of fires marked its former position.

They looked towards the south and towards the north. There was no sign of the army which had camped there the previous night.

"Where could they have disappeared to? Surely they must have moved south to find protection among their followers," one argued.

"Not at all. O'Sullivan is welcome nowhere in the peninsula. He must have moved north," said the other.

"Why north?"

"I do not know."

"We will split up and search in each direction."

"We expose ourselves to danger if we do. Better ride together and move south."

The two spies spurred their horses forward. They travelled for two hours before they came on a peasant gathering firewood. They drew their swords and questioned him.

"Are you certain O'Sullivan did not pass towards the south?"

"Yes. I would have seen him," answered the peasant.

"Then we must turn north. Our day has been wasted."

They began to move north as dusk was falling. Finally they reached a small cabin. Inside a hungry family sat about a boiling pot with expectant eyes.

"What are you eating?" one of the spies asked.

"Roots and berries," the man replied.

"Would you like strong bread?"

"Indeed, kind gentleman, I would."

The spy produced a round loaf of bread. The hungry eyes of the family began to shine.

"You can have it if you give me information."

"What information?" asked the poor man.

"Did a great army pass here?" asked the spy.

"Oh yes. They marched down the coast and then turned left into the mountains."

"And where were they going?"

"No one spoke to me. But they turned left into the mountains. They marched very fast, like as if they were running. In a great hurry they were."

It was sufficient information to satisfy the

spies. They threw the bread into the cabin. The family grabbed it, tore it apart and began to eat.

"Shall we follow them?" one spy asked the other.

"Into the mountains you mean? Yes. But tonight we rest here. The path through the mountains is treacherous, especially at night."

The two spies sat dourly in front of their fire and cursed the fact that they had turned south. They had lost a whole day. They tried to figure out the mind of O'Sullivan Beare. Why did he begin such a treacherous march? He could have submitted to the Queen. He was well regarded and could have become a lord if he took his chances. They fell asleep wondering.

Wilmot, in the inn at the back of the mountain, did not realise that O'Sullivan Beare had marched within three miles of his camp. Great oak forests stood between them. He had spent the morning writing up his notes on the campaign. He was a literate man and took pride in his prose. In London he was well regarded and he hoped some day to publish his account of the wars in Ireland.

On several occasions Wilmot inquired if his spies had returned with information. For a while he wondered if they might have been taken prisoners. But he felt that they would not allow that to happen.

Wilmot could stay no longer at the camp. He planned to spend new year's night at Kenmare with Sir George Carew. He gave orders to his servant.

"As soon as word arrives, have it sent to me at Sir George Carew's residence. I shall spend the next three days there."

As he rode west with an escort of soldiers he wondered why he had not received any information concerning O'Sullivan Beare, but when he entered the fortified castle he left the worries of war behind him.

While O'Sullivan Beare and his followers spent new year's night close to the ancient ruined church of Eachros, Charles Wilmot sat down to a sumptuous supper. In the great oak room he feasted on the finest of meats and drank the best wines. Then he and his host sat in front of the blazing fire and drank mulled punch. It was very late when Charles Wilmot made his way to bed. He felt suddenly war weary. He was tired of the campaign in Ireland. He wished that it could be brought to a quick conclusion. From his bedroom window he looked to the east. Dawn was beginning to break.

5
McCarthy Plans Revenge

he camp stirred as the dawn broke. Soldiers brushed the snow from their mantles and began to move about. Their legs were stiff and so they exercised them in preparation for the march.

Each group huddled close, eating their provisions, conscious of the eyes of others. Soon the food would run out. Hugh ate heartily of meat and bread. He relished his food and he would march a day on his breakfast.

The servants and giollas were rolling up the tents and strapping them to the horses' flanks. They were small tight animals suitable to rugged tracks. However one horse stood out above all the others. This was Cearch, belonging to O'Sullivan Beare. He was a proud animal, white, well-bred and fine-boned. Garech was the giolla in charge of this animal.

Fiach approached him. "You have charge of a fine animal."

Garech looked at the white horse, his eyes bright and eager. "The finest in Munster. But he isn't bred for these rough mountains. It's taking my master into battle he should be. Instead he has to carry a pack. He is nervous. Such work is beneath him."

"Indeed."

"You are with Hugh, the gallowglass?" Garech asked.

"Yes."

"He will protect you well. Have you been to battle with him?"

"Yes. He slaughtered two of Wilmot's men." Fiach explained how they had met in the woods and how they now travelled together.

"I will talk with you later. It is time to form the order of the march. Cearch leads the pack horses." And with that Garech led the white horse into position.

Fiach returned to his sister and mother. They strapped their few possessions on to their horse and moved forward into the long column. Up ahead Hugh prepared to set the pace. They would cross the hills using a pilgrim path.

The sky was grey and angry. A wind blew from the north, cold on the flanks of the hills. The ground over which they passed in the winter morning was wet and boggy. Hugh marched forward at a determined pace. The horses arched their backs and dragged their feet out of the sodden bog. At the wide swamp the cavalcade spread out across the uncertain surface. Giollas cursed their garrans and pulled them forward by the tackling.

Fiach saw it happen. The noble white horse rushed forward and began to sink, quickly at first, then in a long painful movement. The giolla drew at the reins and tried to haul the animal out, crying affectionate words to him. Then the boy jumped into the cold pool and wrapped his arms about the horse. He would have sunk into the pool with the animal had not O'Sullivan Beare caught him by the tunic and drawn him out.

"I betrayed my trust," Garech cried. "I am shamed. You should have let me die with Cearch."

The beautiful horse looked at his master with terror-filled eyes, as if pleading with him. Then the bog slime passed over his mouth, his nostrils and his ears. With a final satiated suck the pool wrinkled and settled. O'Sullivan was choking with sorrow. During days of peace he had raced across summer fields on his noble horse and hunted in the great forests. He was a brother to the wind they said when they watched the smooth flow of his movements. His life had ended as a pack horse and his death had been brutal.

"We must move on. We have no time to lose. There will be days for sorrow later," O'Sullivan told his giolla who still wept.

Garech felt confused, deprived of his position and alone. The other horse boys passed him, some casting rough insults.

"Join us," Fiach offered.

"Very well," Garech said and walked dumbly beside Fiach's horse.

The marching column came through the rough hills and reached the Sullane river. Here the winds were gentler and the ground firm and open. They were edging towards the McCarthy country. There was a sense of danger in the air. The soldiers in the van kept a steady grip on their weapons.

They made their way up the pilgrim path to the shrine of Saint Gobnait. The ruins of a church marked the spot where she had lived in this gentle valley and tended her bees. Having reached the shrine, the marchers knelt on the ground and prayed for a safe passage through the territories of their enemies. There was a low murmur of prayer as people, pressed by hunger and cold, sought relief from the danger about them.

Hugh's eyes had detected movement in the woods. "This is Tadhg McCarthy's country and he has an old score to settle with O'Sullivan. I am sure that he knows already that we are in his territory."

"Then you expect a battle?" Fiach asked.

"It will be more like a skirmish. McCarthy would never face us in open battle. He is a wolf who preys on the flanks of the herd."

Hugh took his sword from the baggage, stood at the rear and called to everyone to resume the march.

Tadhg McCarthy had followed the progress of O'Sullivan Beare; his men brought him a report of O'Sullivan's advance down into the valley.

"They're going towards the shrine of Saint Gobnait to pray," one of his men said.

"He might as well say his last prayer for

when Tadhg McCarthy is finished with him
his head will be spiked above the castle of
Carrigaphoca." McCarthy laughed. His face
was bright with delight. His enemy was
walking into a trap. He would spring upon
him when the time was right.

Tadhg McCarthy had suffered humiliation
at the hands of O'Sullivan Beare who had
attacked his castle and taken his Spanish
gold. Now McCarthy had made his peace with
the Queen, secured a pardon and become a
good subject.

"And read the Queen's words to me, Liam,"
he ordered his scribe. Liam for the fourth
time took the printed notice and read it
aloud.

"And it is also proclaimed that if any
person or persons of what degree or quality
soever that shall into the Lord President
bring the live body of that wicked and
unnatural traitor, Donnell O'Sullyvane, also
O'Sullyvane Beare, shall have the sum of
three hundred pounds."

"Three hundred pounds good solid English
money for the head of an enemy. I'll have his
head spiked before night," McCarthy called
and gulped back his wine. He walked to the
fire and cut a long thin sliver of meat. It

dripped rich juice.

"While O'Sullivan Beare starves, Tadhg McCarthy eats the finest beef. Oh how the great have fallen!"

"Perhaps we should let him pass through the territory," an adviser argued. "He marches with a strong well-trained army."

"We shall never have the chance again. We must take it now. We have old scores to settle. They have marched far and are bound to be hungry and weary. They cannot stand against us," McCarthy replied.

A messenger arrived at the great hall with news that the enemy had left the sacred shrine and were moving down the valley.

"Then move into the woods and prepare to attack. Harass the rear. Harass the rear!"

McCarthy's men moved out of the security of the castle and into the woods on either side of the pass. They could see the long cavalcade ahead.

Suddenly the marchers were attacked from the forest. Spears were thrown into the baggage animals. One horse boy screamed out as the sharp head lodged in his thigh. Instantly Fiach ran forward to where the giolla lay and pulled out the spear.

"I cannot move," the boy cried.

"You must," Fiach warned him. "The horses and the soldiers will trample you to death."

Fiach lifted up the horse boy and pushed him on to the back of one of the pack animals.

There was fear and confusion along the lines as the giollas urged the animals forward. Some of the rear guard raised their muskets and fired into the woods. The attackers slunk into the shelter of the trees only to appear further on.

O'Sullivan Beare was anxious to move forward as quickly as he could. "Abandon all excessive baggage," he ordered. "It is slowing down the march." And with that he passed down the line with his sword and cut the ropes binding the unnecessary baggage.

Women cried out as they watched their possessions fall to the ground. Some tried to retrieve them but to no avail. The soldiers in the rear urged people forward.

Soon the path behind them was littered with baggage. The McCarthys abandoned the chase for the moment and fought amongst themselves for the booty.

"They are carrion." O'Sullivan Beare looked down from the hill at the soldiers fighting like dogs. But they were distracted from their purpose only for a short time and again they advanced. O'Sullivan defended firmly and again the McCarthys were held at bay.

But the pace was telling on the camp followers. The very old abandoned the march. They lay on the side of the road heedless of danger. They wished only to die. The great march was already taking a heavy toll on O'Sullivan's followers.

Hugh moved up through the ranks until he reached O'Sullivan Beare. "It is better to stand and fight. If we continue to push ahead at this pace we will lose more baggage and animals."

He and O'Sullivan moved back to the rear. They waited until Tadhg McCarthy's followers, growing over-confident, were drawn into an open space.

Suddenly the gallowglasses and the kerns turned upon the advancing McCarthys. The surprise tactic worked. The engagement was fast and bloody. Several of McCarthy's men were killed. The rest fled.

"And that is the end of Tadhg McCarthy," O'Sulllivan Beare laughed. "I noted that he was not there to lead his men. He was always a coward and a loud talker."

By now the pressure on the long train had eased but Fiach was worried about his mother. Her eyes were tired and she was breathing heavily. She found the marching difficult. Her life had been one of gentle and comfortable ease. Now she had to push herself beyond the limits of her endurance. She fell forward on the ground.

"I can move no further," she told her son and daughter. "No strength remains in me."

"Mother, you must make a greater effort. The light has almost left the sky. Soon we will surely rest," said Emar.

She and Fiach lifted her on to her feet and, placing her hands on their shoulders, they moved forward into the growing dark.

The marchers were hungry and exhausted. They wished that they could rest but Hugh insisted that they must reach O'Keeffe country.

They moved on and finally they pitched camp at an old church which gave them protection from their enemies. They quickly drew down the camp rods, set them in the earth, secured them with ropes where they crossed and covered them with hides and scraws. They ate what food remained to them. Then, drawing their mantles about them, O'Sullivan's followers fell asleep beneath the rough shelters.

Meanwhile Emar drew the strips of linen off her mother's feet and noticed that blisters were forming on her soles. She took some herbs and rubbed them on the blisters.

"You must try and sleep, mother,"she urged.

"I feel very weary Emar. My body is tired and my spirit seems to lose its courage. I am not like the other women who are used to long journeys on foot."

"You must not talk in that manner. Tomorrow you will feel rested."

Hugh set up a tent where the two women could sleep. Before retiring, he brought them food he had carried in his great satchel of leather.

"You share your last piece of bread with us, Hugh," said the old woman.

"Tomorrow I will find further provisions. Now sleep!" he ordered.

The women crawled into the low barrel-shaped tent and soon fell into a deep sleep.

Others in the camp had not been as fortunate. Their provisions were spent. They went to bed hungry. But fatigue was greater than hunger and they soon slept.

O'Sullivan Beare set sentinels about the camp. There was always the danger of attack. But nobody attacked the camp that night.

In his castle at Carrigaphoca Tadhg McCarthy foamed and frothed. His rage knew no limit.

"Cowards. All cowards!" he shouted to his followers. "You have failed me again. His head should be spiked above my castle. Instead O'Sullivan has his way out of my territory."

6
Crossing the Blackwater

It was half light when the giollas stirred. They went through the camp shaking people awake. Some of the old had died in their sleep and a few soldiers were dead of their wounds. They were hastily buried in shallow graves. Then all fell into line, soldiers going ahead and others taking up the rear. In between stood the garrans with their packs and at the very centre, the most protected of all, the animal which carried O'Sullivan Beare's Spanish gold.

Emar and her mother, refreshed after sleep, stood by the horse and moved forward with the rest. The boots which had been taken from the dead soldiers served their purpose well. They kept out the cold and stood up to the wear of the journey. Others were almost barefoot. The soles of their feet were bleeding and raw. But they had to suppress their pain. There was a hard journey ahead of them and they knew that if they fell by the wayside they would be abandoned. Everyone was now hardened to the demanding conditions of the march.

They moved towards the Blackwater. O'Sullivan Beare avoided Drishane Castle with its tall lookout tower. The long weary line struggled across the Blackwater, oblivious of the cold winter water. The giollas urged the garrans forward, beating them with rods. Finally the long cavalcade reached the far side.

They had moved from the mountains and the land was now flat. This left their flanks exposed. O'Sullivan Beare knew that news of their flight and of the reward for his capture must have reached every dún and castle along the way. His enemies, secure in their castles, could sally against him any time they chose.

"We must move faster," he urged his followers. "If we do not reach secure and protected ground before the night we will be the prey of our enemies."

He passed down the line giving orders, his

eyes sharp, his face tired and drawn.

"Could we not rest a little while?" an old woman begged.

"If you wish to fall out you must take your chances. You may find shelter in some dún," O'Sullivan Beare told her.

"Who wants an old woman who cannot work any more?" she cried.

She continued to plead with him as he passed down the line. Finally she fell on her knees on the hard ground and then lay flat on the cold earth. Nobody had time to lift her up. The cavalcade pushed on. The old woman watched them disappear around a small hill and out of sight.

She lay on the side of the rough road. The earth drew the heat from her body. Two hours later she was dead.

In Liscarroll castle John Barry and Captain Cuffe waited for their messengers to return with definite information. They had sentinels posted on the great towers of the castle which dominated the countryside. They were eager to do battle with O'Sullivan Beare.

"From my knowledge," Captain Cuffe told John Barry, "his army is exhausted. They have been marching at a rapid pace and they lack provisions. Also baggage-animals and campfollowers must be a considerable encumbrance."

Finally one of the messengers arrived with definite news. The army was moving north. Many of the soldiers had been wounded. Some were carried in pallets. Several of the campfollowers had abandoned the march and lay along the route.

"Are they hungry?" Captain Cuffe asked.

"They are marching on empty stomachs. They have had no food for twenty-four hours."

"Then they will have no taste for battle. Let us attack them at the ford of Ballaghan."

The small force gathered in the quadrangle of the castle, eight horsemen and forty footsoldiers. They moved forward through the gate and across the snowbound countryside. They were well prepared to do battle with the straggling army of O'Sullivan Beare.

Fiach and his sister helped their mother along the rough track. Her face was pale and her lips bloodless. Her strength was failing. They wondered how long she could continue. Now that they had come down from the rough countryside the conditions underfoot were not as severe and they moved forward at a regular pace.

Then the train came to a halt. Fiach looked ahead.

"What causes the delay. Are we breaking for a rest?" his mother asked.

They had come to a river and were about to ford when Captain Cuffe and his men appeared on the far side. Instantly the gallowglasses and the kerns fell into formation.

"Take up your positions behind us," Hugh ordered. Emar and her mother drew back a distance and lay on the ground. They looked at the soldiers preparing to engage on either side of the river.

"Where is Fiach?" his mother cried.

"He is with Hugh," Emar answered.

Fiach had followed Hugh, carrying his musket. Hugh had trained him in its use whenever the opportunity arose. It was difficult to load, needing many movements for preparation and firing, but Fiach had almost mastered the technique.

"We must move as close as we can to the enemy," Hugh ordered. "The musket is accurate only within thirty yards."

They moved forward to the bank of the river in a wide line. They set up their muskets and immediately they began to exchange fire. Hugh set up his piece on the branch of a small tree, took careful aim and fired. There was a puff of smoke which held the air for a moment. Fiach watched a soldier gaze incredulously across the river, place his hands on his chest and fall forwards on his face.

It took Fiach a minute to reload the musket. His fingers were nervous as he put the powder in place. Hugh took the musket, placed it in position and fired again.

"A wasted shot," he commented.

As he was about to reload the musket one of the soldiers beside him was hit in the head. Fiach looked at the gaping hole in the forehead and the spongy matter which trickled down the face. Hugh, unmoved by death, commented: "A worthy shot!"

O'Sullivan Beare moved up and down the long line lending support to the musketeers. The engagement continued for an hour. Then Captain Cuffe and his men withdrew from the far side of the river. The troops of O'Sullivan Beare were too weary to cheer. Instead they quickly buried the dead in shallow graves. The wounded soldiers where rapidly bandaged and those who could not walk placed upon rough litters.

The skirmish gave Emar's mother some time to recover. When she rose again she felt a little stronger. She moved forward with the rest across the cold river, unmindful of the freezing waters. They climbed up the opposite bank, fell into formation and continued the march.

Many of the soldiers were beginning to complain. The camp followers were a burden upon them. They were holding up the progress of the march. They pushed them forward at a rapid rate, cursing the stragglers. Several fell to the side and abandoned the march.

Now they were moving through open country. The sky was low and grey and angry. A cold wind was blowing from the north, carrying sleet into their faces. The light was weak. Everywhere the countryside looked bleak and empty. But on several occasions they noticed soldiers at a distance, mounted on horses and surveying their progress like wolves on the flanks of a moving herd, waiting to pounce.

It was towards evening that they moved across the flanks of the Ballyhoura mountains. Great oak woods grew on the flanks offering protection. They moved along the edge of these woods feeling more secure than on the flatlands of Tipperary.

They felt relieved as they reached Ardpatrick. It was a deserted place, a vast solitude, free from the prying eyes of enemies. It was also a sanctuary. Here O'Sullivan Beare could pray and rest and prepare for a quick dash across the plains of Limerick.

"We are very far from home," his mother said to Fiach when she lay upon the ground. "I feel that I shall never reach the end of this journey. Leave me here to die in peace for I cannot make any more effort."

"You must continue. Have you seen how Dermot O'Sullivan marches? He is seventy years of age and he has not complained," Fiach told her.

Their conversation was broken by the arrival of Hugh. He praised Fiach for his courage under fire. He opened his bag, produced a rough piece of bread and offered it to Fiach's mother.

"But you have not eaten today, Hugh."

"True but tomorrow I shall fill my stomach. We march through Limerick and although it is filled with enemies it is also filled with food. I shall fill my stomach and my satchel," he laughed.

The stores of food had run out, but people were too weary to complain. They rolled themselves in their mantles and fell asleep. Even the guards could not stay awake. They slept at their posts and left the camp unguarded.

That night a great storm blew up. It raged through the branches of the trees. But the followers of O'Sullivan Beare slept deeply.

7
The Black Knight

he camp stirred before
dawn. In the lonesome
valley they had some
protection from the enemy and many wished
to linger there and regain their strength. By
now their numbers had been reduced to eight
hundred. Many had died from exhaustion,
and others of their wounds. Some had
abandoned the march and sought refuge in
the countryside.

O'Sullivan Beare was deep in thought as
he walked through the camp, noting the
condition of his army and followers. He had
kept to the pilgrim paths where he was
certain of a clear passage. He had forced his
people to march across the mountains,
knowing that many would die on the way. He
was determined to drive his way through

Ireland and find hospitality in the north.

His mind was troubled. He often sat alone brooding over the past few weeks. He had abandoned his own people. Had he remained in the peninsula, perhaps help might have come from Spain. Now he had left his people exposed and Wilmot would swing down the peninsula and slaughter them. It was a savage war in which few prisoners were taken.

Hugh the Gallowglass visited the tent of O'Sullivan Beare. "Today we pass through open country again, my lord. We move into the territory of the White Knight. By now news of your flight will have reached Limerick. We can expect opposition all the way."

"Then have the musketeers clean their weapons. And we must move quickly at all times and never give the enemy time to regroup. If we take a stand it must be to our advantage," said O'Sullivan Beare.

"I must draw your attention to the shortage of food. Last night most people went to bed hungry. What shall we do?"

"Live off the land. I regard everyone through whose territory we pass as a sworn enemy. They know I carry gold and that I bear a price upon my head. We must find provisions."

"Very well. I shall relay the orders to all the men." Hugh passed back through the camp. He gathered the soldiers about him and gave them a description of the country through which they would now pass.

The order went out to fall into line. Fiach and Emar helped their mother into position. Her face was drawn and her body feeble. They were afraid that her spirit was failing.

Hugh was quick to notice her condition. "Today your mother rides the garran. Make it comfortable for her."

Her children placed the camp cloth on the back of the animal and Hugh lifted her on to its back.

"You are a kind man Hugh. You have more than a soldier's heart," she said.

"Thank you lady," he bowed, and then took up his position at the head of the march.

Quickly they marched out of the wood and down towards the hostile plains of Limerick.

Fiach left the care of his mother to Emar. He felt that he must be close to Hugh. He was his giolla and he must have Hugh's great axe ever at the ready. He ran forward and marched beside the enormous soldier. Hugh stood a head above the rest of the men. His massive thighs carried him forward at a tremendous pace and he never grew weary nor complained.

Now they were on the flat lands where cattle fattened during summer days on lush grass. But there was no sign of any animals. It was obvious that news had passed from dún to castle that O'Sullivan Beare was marching through the countryside without provisions.

The frozen earth beneath them was as hard as iron. They marched without words. Only the sound of their breaths and of their feet broke the silence of the place. On each side the land stretched, open and unprotecting.

"I am uncomfortable," Hugh muttered. "I feel that eyes are preying upon us. I feel that this will be the worst of days for us. I can sense it in the still air."

And then a figure appeared in the distance, out of the greyish winter haze. He rode a black horse and he wore black armour. He stood before them for some time. Then, as quickly and silently as he appeared, he disappeared again.

"It is the Black Knight," the soldiers

whispered fearfully. "He brings death with him. He is soldier and devil."

The word passed down the line that the Black Knight had appeared on the horizon.

"He brings only death. He brings only death," was repeated again and again.

And then the knight appeared on the right flank, observing them from a distance as he sat rigidly upon his horse.

"He is nothing but a man like the rest of us," Hugh roared. "He bleeds like the rest of us. He bears my sword wounds upon his body. I know him of old."

"When did you exchange blows with him?" Fiach asked.

Hugh's face turned dark and for a moment Fiach thought he would raise his great hand and hit him. However he stayed his anger. "March!" he ordered. "Keep your eyes sharp. Expect an attack from either side at any moment."

He had no sooner uttered the word when a musket shot rang out. The sound seemed to hang in the air for a moment. A soldier marching beside Hugh put his hand to his neck. Blood oozed through his fingers and ran down his chest. He reeled away from the marching column and fell dead.

"Keep marching. Keep marching!" O'Sullivan Beare called, moving up towards the head of the column. His eyes were sharp and piercing and there was nervous anger in his voice. Danger now surrounded them on every side. The Black Knight had made his dread appearance. And they were in the land of the White Knight, whose followers were gathering under Conn Gibbons.

Conn Gibbons felt secure at Hospital. The town held a key position controlling the wide fertile plains. It was well fortified and provided. He knew that his men could winter there in comfort.

Gibbons, now fifty years of age, owed loyalty to the White Knight who at that moment was campaigning in Kerry. Gibbons's fortunes had improved during the Elizabethan wars. His master had played the game of war well. He had picked the winning side and was part of the new order. Gibbons now owned land and held positions of importance while O'Sullivan Beare had backed the losing side and was fleeing out of Munster with his followers, desperately trying to hold them together.

Conn Gibbons had sent out his scouts

before dawn to discover what they could concerning the fugitives. Now, as he sat in the comfort of the castle drinking mulled wine, he listened to what his scouts had to say. Gibbons had a passion for chess. He possessed a set of precious pieces cast in silver and in gold. He carried them with him on all his campaigns. Now he had them set out on the table in front of him. The silver pieces arranged in a line represented O'Sullivan Beare's followers. The royal pieces were set in the rear and in the front of the line. The pawns represented the baggage animals and the camp followers.

"Where did they camp last night?" Gibbons asked.

"In the glens at Ardpatrick," a scout replied.

"And you say they are starving?"

"Yes. We captured one of the stragglers, an old man. He gave us all the information we needed. They have not eaten for forty-eight hours, are weary from marching and are heading for Connacht."

"And the pace of the march?"

"Thirty miles a day," the scout replied.

"That pace cannot be sustained. O'Sullivan has undertaken an impossible task. Soon the

Shannon will present a barrier to him and no one will ferry him across." Conn Gibbons moved some chessmen and then sipped his mulled wine.

"He moves quickly because there is a price on his head and he fears for his chest of Spanish gold. O'Sullivan is only a twilight lord now. His power has passed and with every step he takes away from his lands he becomes less a lord and more of a fugitive. He is fair game."

"Where will we give battle?" one of his men asked.

"Let us take advantage of our position," replied Gibbons. We will harass him. Our horses are fresh and we shall use our musketeers. Attack their flanks. Let the sorties be quick and deadly. Attack the centre. That is their weak link. If we can split them into small groups then we can slaughter them at leisure."

By now Gibbons had set out his golden pieces to the left and right of the silver ones. With quick movements of his fingers he indicated how he intended the battle to be fought.

The orders were given. By ten o'clock his troops were ready in the square of the town.

He directed them out into the countryside covered with snow and moved them towards their positions.

When Conn Gibbons reached the right flank of O'Sullivan's straggling train he watched fascinated. The enemy seemed voiceless. They moved resolutely through the snow. Here and there wounded soldiers were carried on rough pallets. A huge gallowglass led the van. Gibbons recognised him from reputation.

Gibbons gave the signal for his horse soldiers to attack. He would test the strength of his enemy. He raised his hand and ordered his men forward. They drew their swords and charged.

As Hugh the Gallowglass looked into the winter haze he saw the horse soldiers moving forward. Quickly he ordered the musketeers to take their positions. Fiach, who had marched beside him carrying the musket and tripod, handed it to Hugh who set it in the snow and prepared for the attack. When the enemy were within range, Hugh fired. A rider fell from his saddle onto the snow and his horse bolted.

Musket fire rang out along the line and

Conn Gibbons, cursing his mistake, withdrew to a safer distance and used his musketeers.

The wounded cried out for help but O'Sullivan's train moved on, deaf to their pleas. Some of the enemy came forward to slit their throats and rob them of their possessions.

"Can you hold on mother?" Emar cried when the enemy musketeers fired indiscriminately into the centre of the marchers and the garrans, sensing danger, began to bolt.

"I will do my best," she moaned.

Emar could give her little comfort. All about them people were wounded but carried on as best they could until, exhausted by loss of blood, they fell on the ground and were abandoned by the advancing marchers.

Meanwhile, O'Sullivan Beare lamented the clear day which gave the enemy the advantage. They could move freely along his flanks and pick off his best men. Now he ordered his musketeers to return fire. They quickly set up their weapons and with accurate aim began to hit back at the enemy. As soon as they had discharged their muskets, they reloaded them and moved forward into a new position, so keeping up with the pace of the march.

O'Sullivan looked at the sky. He prayed that snow would fall but his prayers were not granted and he had to fight a running battle for eight hours.

The attacks settled into a regular pattern. It was a bloody test of courage but towards the end of the day the enemy began to falter. The worst of the battle was over. It had been fought at a high cost. The route lay littered with the dead.

Finally O'Sullivan and his people reached a large ring fort. They struggled through the opening and threw themselves on the banks too exhausted to speak. But the giollas were quick to start fires and people drew near them, their eyes staring at the centre of heat. When they had some warmth in their bodies they began to think of food. With their knives they dug up the ground in search of roots. As quickly as they discovered them they cleaned them and ate. It was rough sustenance but welcome to hungry stomachs.

Later in doleful groups they settled to sleep. Here and there the wounded cried out for aid. But the women were too exhausted to help and during the night many of them died.

That night Conn Gibbons looked grimly at his chessmen set out upon a board. His tactics had had not succeeded. He had failed to capture either O'Sullivan Beare or the Spanish gold. He had not prevented the refugees marching through the land of his master though all the advantages had stood with him. Not even the warm food which the servant women carried to him could bring him comfort.

8
Fiach Kills a Man

efore Fiach fell asleep
that night he thought of
how the march had
changed him. His muscles had hardened. He
could now move as rapidly as the best
soldiers. He had shown courage in battle. He
had stood with Hugh and loaded his musket
while men fell dead around him. He had
learned how to keep cool under the most
extreme circumstances. And Hugh had
trained him in the use of a short sword and
dagger.

Fiach was dreaming pleasantly when
Hugh shook him awake. "Time to break
camp. The dawn will soon be here."

Fiach stood up and shook the frost rime off
his mantle. He looked about him. The camp
was stirring. The soldiers were burying

corpses in a shallow grave, something they attended to each morning before the others woke.

O'Sullivan, his bearing noble and his voice controlled, surveyed the conditions of the camp. He knew that his people would soon suffer from starvation. Men and women could only march a certain distance without food and his followers had been forced to march too far.

"We must obtain food before the day is out, Hugh," he said to the gallowglass.

"I know this region," said Hugh. "I marched through it with O'Donnell. If there are provisions to be found anywhere then we will find them at Donohill which is defended by the O'Dwyers. Mind you, I do not think they can be persuaded to share with us."

"Then we must take Donohill by force. I will not have the people starve. Let it be known that we will eat before the sun sets," replied O'Sullivan decisively.

He passed among his followers. They were gathering their belongings, bundling them together and strapping them on to the backs of the garrans. They were tired and weary and desperately needed food.

Meanwhile Fiach, having helped his

mother on to the back of the horse, walked to
the rear with Hugh. The marchers began to
make their way across the flatlands towards
Donohill.

Finally Donohill stood before them. It was
a man-built hill and well fortified. The incline
to the palisade on top was steep and almost
impossible to climb. Behind the palisade and
towering above them O'Sullivan could see the
thatched roofs of the storerooms which
sheltered supplies of food.

Within the fort the O'Dwyers expected an
attack. News had been sent to them that
O'Sullivan was crossing the Limerick plain on
his way to the Shannon. He was without
provisions and would obviously attempt to
capture the wooden fortress.

"Wait until they attempt the slope,"
O'Dwyer ordered. He watched from behind
the fortifications the approach of the
fugitives. He was surprised at how firmly
they marched. Well disciplined kerns and
gallowglass were armed with muskets. The
reports O'Dwyer had received from his
neighbours had been inaccurate.

O'Sullivan's men advanced towards the hill
and formed a circle about it. This divided the
attention of the defenders who watched with

growing fear as the musketeers went through
the drill of loading their weapons. Powder
was poured and the wads and bullets
rammed home. Then they set the muskets on
their rests and aimed, waiting for O'Sullivan
Beare to give the order to fire.

At a signal from O'Sullivan a volley of
shots rang out. Splinters of wood flew from
the top of the palisade. O'Sullivan's men
moved up the slope, clawing at the earth for
support, sliddering back and then dragging
themselves forward again. Hunger
strengthened their determination. They must
have food or die.

As one line of musketeers reloaded their
weapons another line fired and a volley rang
out. The soldiers and the giollas were panting
as they crawled up the steep slope. Two were
killed and rolled down to the base of the hill.
The rest finally reached the doors. With axes
and swords they hacked at the timbers,
hunger forcing them forward. Then they
pushed against the weakened doors which
sprung open to reveal a body of armed men
ready to engage them.

It was the first time Fiach witnessed Hugh
in a close engagement. With his great sword
the gallowglass hacked through the guards as

if they were straw men. They fell back in terror at his immense size, before the accuracy of his strokes.

"Kill! Kill!" Hugh roared in blood lust. Even those who knelt and cringed for mercy were slain.

All over the enclosure the battle raged. A man groaned in agony as he clutched a fatal wound. "Put him out of his misery," Hugh ordered Fiach. "I have trained you for moments like this. You are not playing with a toy sword."

Fiach raised the sword above the dying man whose eyes were pleading for help but he could not bring it down upon the unfortunate. Grasping his hands, Hugh made Fiach drive his sword into the man's chest, and then pull out the bloody blade. Fiach felt disgust pass through his body.

"This is not a time for mercy," Hugh roared. Let us see what food lies in the stores."

With his sword the gallowglass cut the leather hinges and opened the doors. The starving soldiers ran in to where piles of bread stood in baskets. They took up the griddled oaten bread and began to eat ravenously. Hugh ate savagely, swallowing huge mouthfuls of food and drinking from a barrel of beer he had opened. When he was satiated he stuffed oaten bread into his satchel and into his great jerkin.

"Fill this bag with food for your mother and sister," he ordered Fiach. "I will fill a sack with grain. It should sustain us for several days."

By now Hugh's battle anger had cooled. He ordered the men to gather as much grain as they could carry and bring it down to the people at the base of the hill.

As Fiach made his way to his mother, he felt weak at the thought of the man he had helped to kill. One moment the man's eyes were alive with fright and then there was a splurt of blood along the blade and the man was dead. It had been a terrible experience.

Fiach's sister and his mother were waiting for him anxiously. They had kept their eyes on the door of the fort, hardly expecting to see him alive again. When they saw him emerge they threw their arms about each other in delight. Fiach made his way towards them clutching the food. Finally he reached the place where his mother and sister sat.

"I have brought you food," he told them as he handed them each a precious oatmeal cake. They began to eat. When Fiach saw the relief on their faces he felt proud that he had taken part in the battle. They ate slowly, enjoying the strong healthy taste of the food. When they were finished he offered them two more cakes which they also ate.

"I will pack the rest with the baggage. They will be welcome tonight," he said.

"Are you wounded?" his mother asked, noticing the blood on his clothes.

"No," Fiach said but did not offer to tell her what had happened at the fort.

She, realising he was hiding something, asked: "Did somebody pay for this bread with their lives?"

Then he told her what happened during the battle.

"You are not yet a man but you have already become a soldier. My young boy has become a soldier. We indeed live in desperate times."

9
The Mother's Dream

hat night, lying in the
low tent beside her
daughter, Emar's sad
mother dreamt of her life in the castle close to
the sea. It was summer time and the gentle
winds from the sea were filled with the tang
of the salt and the seaweed. Standing on the
tower she could see the small currachs
fishing close to the shore and in the distance
the great sails of a trading ship carrying rich
cargoes from Spain. The ships carried gifts to
the castle; fine silks from the cities of the
east, spices for meats and wines of the best
quality. The sea captains were welcomed and
feasted in the castle. The servants carried
dishes of fish, briskets of boiled beef and
shoulders of mutton to the great oak tables.
Her husband was dressed in his finest

costume and her young children had been
permitted to gaze at the great feast from the
gallery. She wore her most elegant dress
edged with fine lace. Later the harpers came
and played to the company. The sweet music
echoed from the vaulted roof and had a fairy
quality which filled the mind with delightful
pictures. The summer days by the sea seemed
endless and sweet.

Then she dreamt she sailed to Spain and
walked through streets where high buildings
of red sandstone rose on either side, where
women stood on balconies waving their fans
and gossiping. Courtyards were secret places
of shadow, where water played from
ornamental fountains and passed down in
light cascades over the lips of basins to quiet
pools below. As night fell she listened to the
soothing noise of the courtyard fountains.
They carried the mind down into sleep.

"It is time to waken, mother. Another day is
breaking," Emar's voice called.

Now awake, her mother looked at the
soiled cover of the tent. She wished that she
could return to sleep. She wished that she
could have the comfort of a warm fire and the
taste of good food on her tongue.

"I was dreaming of Spain," she told her daughter. "I was again walking through the streets of Cordova."

Her daughter looked at the frail face of her mother and felt sorrow in her heart. She believed that her mother was dying and had no wish to live any longer or to continue the march which seemed endless.

Emar took the remaining oatcake, broke a fragment off and fed it to her mother who ate it slowly. She kept feeding her until the whole cake had been consumed.

"Have you no food for yourself, Emar?" the mother asked.

"Yesterday I ate more than my share. I feel strong."

"You need the food more than I. You should have eaten it. Soon I will not need food."

"You must not give up hope. Shortly we will pass over the Shannon and find hospitality."

But Emar knew that the march had taken a heavy toll of her mother. Responsibility had passed on to Emar's shoulders. The journey had changed her and she no longer needed the protection of her mother. She had become a young woman.

Emar quickly dismantled the small tent and having bundled it up, strapped it to the garran. She would not have attempted such heavy work at the beginning of the march.

The land about them was rougher now and the Slievefelim mountains stood on the left, their flanks covered with heavy falls of snow. All waited in silence for the signal. Hugh called out the orders. The cavalcade moved forward.

O'Sullivan's band moved north in a determined manner. The food which they had captured at Donohill fort had now been consumed and after three hours of marching they began to complain to O'Sullivan Beare that they were again hungry. They could no longer continue to march at such a pace.

But their complaints were short lived. They realised that they were in Ormond's territory and that his forces blocked the way. Their hunger was quickly forgotten as they fell into battle order.

O'Sullivan Beare took up his position before his men. He possessed a stubborn bravery and he was determined not to be beaten. "Let us show Ormond's troops what we are made of. We will not wait for them.

Let us attack."

He signalled to the musketeers to fire. The volley rang out and some of Ormond's men fell. Before the enemy could recover from the surprise, O'Sullivan Beare attacked. Strength seemed to surge through his tired men as they pushed forward. Quickly they engaged the superior enemy who, completely taken by surprise at the ferocity of the attack, turned and fled, leaving several dead and dying.

The battle had taken its toll of O'Sullivan Beare's troops but he did not have time to weep over the dead or the dying. He ordered the cavalcade to move forward.

"These are hard and savage times," Hugh said to Fiach, who marched beside him. "At another time we could have buried the dead and attended to the wounded but we must press on towards the Shannon. We must cross the great river."

Later in the day, O'Sullivan Beare ordered the cavalcade to halt. He called aside Thomas Burke and Daniel O'Malley.

"I have decided to split up our forces. I am placing sixty of my best men under your command. We are desperately in need of food. Sweep in a half circle in that direction and join us five miles further along the route with whatever food you discover along the way."

The sixty soldiers set off briskly up into the hills in search of food. As O'Sullivan Beare watched them go and looked at his own depleted force, he wondered if he had made a mistake. Because of the desperate food shortage he had divided his force.

But the foraging party had been spotted. The people who lived on the side of Slieve Felim had experience of armies marching through their territories. Earlier O'Donnell had plundered their cattle and burned their houses and left them destitute. That had hardened them against those who would live off their land. They had watched O'Donnell's men return from Kinsale and slaughtered the weakened army. Now they prepared to engage the forces of O'Sullivan Beare. They lay in the cold above the pass and watched Thomas Burke and Daniel O'Malley march into the trap. The foraging party was taken by surprise and could not get themselves into order. The attackers advanced down the valley sides, their pikes set before them. The foragers, packed together, could not use their weapons. In the first charge several were killed including Daniel O'Malley. The rest managed to hack their way out of the glen and flee. O'Sullivan Beare, for the first time since the march had begun, had suffered a serious defeat.

As soon as the first fugitive arrived with news of the defeat, O'Sullivan ordered his army to change course. He quickly reached the glen and saw the carnage. It had been a waste of fighting men and a foolish, costly mistake. The soldiers buried their comrades, cursing O'Sullivan Beare for his rash mistake.

As they finished covering their comrades with cold earth, Thomas Burke blundered towards them. He had been captured by the enemy but had succeeded in escaping and running for his life. He was without pike, sword and dagger. O'Sullivan Beare greeted him coldly and straightaway gave the order to reform and move on.

Dispirited, his men fell into line and marched northwards once more. They finally arrived at the village of Latteragh, a place of pilgrimage where Saint Odhran had once set up a small church. Here, on the eve of the Epiphany, O'Sullivan Beare knelt on the sacred ground and prayed for the souls of those who had fallen during the day. He had followed the pilgrim paths since he left Glengarriff and at each shrine he had prayed for the souls of his dead. He wondered how many more days he could hold out against weather and against enemies who surrounded him on every side.

Near the churchyard where O'Sullivan's followers now camped stood the castle of the de Marisco family. From the battlements soldiers discharged musketfire into the graveyard. But soon it grew dark and the firing ceased.

O'Sullivan's people had taken up protective positions in the lee of the walls of the churchyard. Sentinels were posted and stood in readiness on the perimeter of the camp. O'Sullivan's followers knew that the Shannon was a day's march north. They wished that they had already crossed over the wide river to Connacht.

10
The Black Knight Again

he great castle emerged from the darkness above the church enclosure and became a menacing presence in the growing light. From behind the broken wall of the churchyard O'Sullivan's followers looked at the turrets and saw the barrels of muskets. Orders were given by Hugh. Quietly the musketeers prepared their muskets; shots rang out and the muskets in the embrasures of the castle were withdrawn. However during the second exchange three young men were mortally wounded. Eventually the church enclosure was abandoned and O'Sullivan's men assembled out of musket range.

De Marisco from his battlement had watched the retreat of O'Sullivan Beare's followers with interest. He stroked his black beard with pleasure as some unfortunate giolla keeled over and fell to the ground. The figures beneath him were as insignificant as pawns on a chessboard. Even their cries of pain were weakened by distance. He watched the pathetic creatures gather their possessions and strap them to the garrans and then flee into the distance. He looked down at the old church enclosure. Twelve people lay dead on the withered grasses. His musketeers had been tolerably accurate. He called for his servant to bring him some French wine. Drinking from his ornamental goblet and dressed in warm sheepskin, he watched the famished line of refugees disappear into the white winter mist.

That night the Black Knight sought hospitality from de Marisco. He rode up to the gate in his Spanish armour, his horse breathing heavily. De Marisco did not refuse him entrance, though there was something sinister about his presence.

Beside the Black Knight rode a short, barrel-chested mute. His eyes bulged and his face was heavy and ugly. He wore a rough stocking of wool on his bulbous head beneath his helmet. He dismounted and bent down beside the Black Knight, who used his back as a step. The Black Knight entered the great hall and sat beside de Marisco.

"I accept the hospitality of your castle. I have been turned away along the route but I have placed my curse upon those who refused me shelter," he said in a hollow voice.

"And how shall they die?" de Marisco asked.

"From fever or at the hands of assassins. But their deaths will be slow and lingering."

The knight ate sparingly while his man ate ravenously.

"He is a peasant and should be quartered with the pigs. He is a Spaniard. I saved him from the gallows and he has been my man ever since."

The Black Knight called out in Spanish and the mute stopped eating. He looked at his master with fear in his bulging eyes and left the room.

"We shall play chess before I sleep, de Marisco. A warlike game pleases my mind. Have the pieces set out."

The members of de Marisco's family gathered about the chess players. De Marisco, who was skilful at the game, knew he had met his master when they had begun the middle game. The Black Knight had an agile mind and could anticipate all his moves. The end game was slow and deadly. The Black Knight toyed with de Marisco; then as the torches flickered he brought the game to a rapid close.

"And in the same manner will the gallowglass die."

"Who?" de Marisco asked.

"The gallowglass who heads the march of O'Sullivan Beare. I will wait until he is weak, then I will move upon him. We have to meet in a final encounter."

"Why must you waste your talents on such a common soldier?" de Marisco asked.

"When your retainers have left the hall I shall tell you," the knight said.

De Marisco ordered all those in the hall to retire. The torches flickered, throwing ghostly shadows. The two men sat in large chairs in front of the dying fire.

"Once upon a time I was the greatest of knights. I travelled to Jerusalem. I fought on the Spanish borders. I was the most elegant and accomplished of men. Look at me now!" and with that the Black Knight pushed up his visor. De Marisco was appalled at what he

saw. One eye was white and sightless. The
left side of his face was scarred. The Black
Knight drew down the visor again in shame.

"The Gallowglass maimed me many years
ago. Now we must fight in a final battle. One
of us must die. Goodnight!" The knight left
for his chamber.

Next morning before daybreak the Black
Knight departed from the castle and de
Marisco never saw him again.

The straggling column following O'Sullivan
made its way northwards. The march had
taken a terrible toll. Each hour somebody,
weakened by hunger, fell by the side.
Everywhere enemies seemed to lurk, fresh
and fed and able to take advantage of the
tired marchers.

Ahead lay the flat lands which bordered
the Shannon. Hugh hoped that within two
days they would pass across the river to the
safety of Connacht. The landscape was now
flat and tedious. There were few landmarks
from which to take direction. But Hugh had a
sure instinct and he marched forward with
determination and certainty.

"Two more days and we will be in
Connacht. There at least we can be sure of

some comfort."

"Are you certain that we shall find refuge there?" Fiach asked.

"I am never certain of anything. These are strange times. People change their allegiance".

For the moment however they were granted some peace. O'Sullivan Beare decided that they should rest that night at Lackeen. It was a place of pilgrimage. They would rest there before their final push across the Shannon. Beyond the river he expected fewer attacks.

A white winter mist reduced visibility. A thin cover of snow lay on the hard ground. Only the sound of neighing garrans and of marching feet broke the silence. People remained mute. It helped reserve their strength. They marched mechanically and without thought towards the Shannon. They were hungry. Leather shoes had worn thin and so they walked on bare feet. Their soles were raw and bleeding and in some cases frostbitten.

"Will it ever end," a woman cried as she stumbled forward. "We should never have set out on this madcap march. O'Sullivan deserted his own."

She echoed the feelings of others. Had they realised how long the journey would be and how hard the conditions, they would have remained on Beare peninsula. But now they were committed to a white purgatory.

An elderly man who had marched vigorously for many days suddenly clasped his chest, let out a gasp and fell dead in front of Emar. His wife pulled him aside. She cried over his dead body. The train passed by her. She watched it move further and further from her. Too late, she realised that she could not catch up. She rushed forward making a desperate effort, but fell in the heavy snow. Nobody noticed her. All were looking doggedly north.

It was evening when they reached Lackeen. They gathered about the place of pilgrimage and pitched their tents. Soon they had collected enough firewood to build some camp fires. They sat about them trying to put warmth into cold bodies.

O'Sullivan Beare called Hugh aside.

"I wish you to ride forward and see if you can hire a boatman to ferry us across the Shannon. We have gold in plenty and we will pay him well."

"Very well. I shall bring Fiach with me. He has keen eyes and can keep a sharp watch about him."

"Here is some gold," O'Sullivan said, handing him a purse of money. "Use it to the best advantage."

Hugh returned to Fiach, Emar and their mother. He explained to them that he must ride out of the camp and wished Fiach to accompany him.

"Take care of my son," Fiach's mother said. "He is all that I have left to protect me." Her voice was weak and ever day her strength failed a little more.

Hugh was worried about her health but he hid his fears. He mounted the horse they had captured and drew Fiach up behind him. Hugh carried his great sword and his dagger. They waved to Emar and her mother and moved out into the winter evening. The hoof sounds on the snow sounded like drum beats. They journeyed for some three miles until they came upon clumps of sally bushes.

"We have reached the Shannon," Hugh said. He pushed the horse slowly forward. Before them were frozen reeds, and, stretching into the distance, the dark waters of Lough Derg. They turned right and made their way along the bank towards the district of Redwood where the MacEgan castle stood. They saw a light in a small rush cabin close to the shore. They dismounted and stood at the door. Within sat a woman who drew her children to her and clasped them in fear.

"We mean no harm," Hugh assured her. "We come in search of a ferryman who will carry us across the Shannon."

"Then no ferryman will you find for miles," the woman answered. "They have been warned by MacEgan to remove their boats downstream so that O'Sullivan Beare cannot use them. This very day they set off downriver."

It was disastrous news. Hugh felt anger grow in him. They were trapped just when they hoped they could take the final step towards freedom. He cursed MacEgan in his castle at Redwood. "May he choke on his fine food and may no good luck attend him. He has condemned us to death. Let us return to the camp. Do not breath a word to anyone. It is only for the ears of O'Sullivan Beare."

O'Sullivan had finished praying at the sacred place and was sitting in his camp when they brought him the news. He bowed his head in despair. The Shannon had become an impassable barrier.

11
Crossing the Shannon

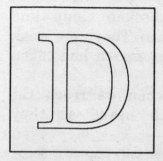

onnchadh MacEgan stood on the battlements of his castle at Redwood close to the Shannon. He was the Queen's sheriff for the area and his allegiance was soon to be put to the test. Two days previously he had received information that O'Sullivan Beare would cross the Shannon close to Redwood Castle. MacEgan dispatched a message to all the boatmen that they would forfeit their lives if they helped the fugitive.

Now he watched the line of soldiers and camp followers march in the direction of his castle. He made a quick check of their numbers; a little over five hundred people. They marched in good order and it was obvious to MacEgan's trained eye that his men were no match for the tested soldiers of

O'Sullivan Beare. He would keep to the castle for the moment and observe the fugitives from the battlements.

That morning the army and followers of O'Sullivan Beare had broken camp and moved towards the Shannon. They were weak with hunger and the long march had taken toll of their energies.

"What shall we do when we reach the Shannon, Hugh?" Fiach asked as they marched along.

"I know not. Perhaps we can capture some craft. We cannot turn about now. There must be some solution to our problem."

Fiach turned the problem about in his mind. He could find no answer either.

He left the van and returned to see his mother. She looked very frail and she had an arm over the shoulder of Emar, who was supporting her body.

"She must ride the horse," Fiach told his sister. He helped his mother on to the back of the horse. Her face was expressionless. Her head bobbed up and down to the movement of the horse. Fiach and Emar looked at each other. They knew their mother was dying. Tears started to their eyes but they did not weep.

Soon Redwood castle towered above O'Sullivan's followers. They kept a safe distance from the musketeers on the battlements. The soldiers hoped there would not be a sally from the castle. They were weary from the constant battles and even Hugh seemed to have lost the spring to his step.

Hugh decided that they should march towards the forests in the curve formed by the Brosna and the Shannon. At least they would have the protection of the oak trees while they rested.

When they reached the shelter of the forest O'Sullivan Beare addressed them. He explained that they were now cornered and that there was no means of escape.

"Have we come this far from home to die in a strangers territory?" one of his followers asked. "Perhaps we should have stayed in the Caha mountains instead of undertaking this mad journey through Ireland."

It was the first time that O'Sullivan's judgement and authority were challenged. Despair filled his eyes.

At this point Dermot of Dursey stepped forward and took up position beside

O'Sullivan Beare. He was uncle to the leader and now an old man of seventy. He had the body of a much younger man and he had marched the long distance without complaint. He had scaled castle walls, had survived close combat and had been wounded many times. He spoke in a deep, gravelly voice.

"I have not come this far to lie down by the Shannon side and give up. We have beaten off enemies during the course of six days, we have endured hunger and cold and we have not complained. This is the first secure position we have held. Behind us are two rivers which protect us and the woods about us give us further protection. We can rest and eat here and then we can sail across the river." With that he told them of the plan which had formed in his mind.

O'Sullivan Beare spoke again. "It must be attempted. We have no other way of escaping across the river. We hold a good defensive position for the moment but MacEgan could quickly gather a large army and we would be slaughtered in these woods. We will follow the instructions of Dermot of Dursey."

With their great axes the kerns and gallowglasses set about cutting down trees. They sought out straight ash trees which they quickly felled, pointed and drove into the ground to form a palisade. As soon as it was finished all gathered within. Soon warm fires gave them protection and comfort.

One of the camp followers had been a butcher who had prepared the finest meats for the tables of Dermot of Dursey. Now he put his skills to a more practical use. While others held a horse down, he cut the vein in his neck and blood spouted forth. People drank the rich blood, calling out in joy that their lives had been saved.

But Emar's and Fiach's mother refused. "I could not drink it, I'm afraid. I was well brought up and I find it offensive."

"But you must eat, mother," Fiach insisted.

"No horse meat, Fiach. Please do no ask me to eat horse meat," she pleaded.

But no fine sentiments stirred in others. The horse was skinned carefully, then dismembered and the pieces carried to the fire. They were cut into slivers, set on pointed rods and roasted. Soon the heavy scent of cooking horse-flesh filled the woods.

Fiach protested when Hugh lead their horse away for slaughter. "How will my mother travel through Connacht? She is frail and cannot walk anymore."

"I have my orders," said Hugh, and pushing Fiach aside he brought the horse to the far corner of the palisade where it was slaughtered, skinned and dismembered.

Fiach stood alone. Tears filled his eyes. He had no wish to join the others. He began to hate the march and the leaders who had brought them out of Beare peninsula.

Now, with everyone well-fed, the men set about chopping down the trees which would make the boat. Dermot of Dursey was about to organise men into work teams when the first disagreement occurred. The O'Malleys, who were Mayo mercenaries, refused to join with the others. They had remained apart from the outset.

"We are seafaring people," they told Dermot of Dursey. "We can build a craft which will carry us across more rapidly. Moreover it can be built with less effort."

Dermot of Dursey suppressed his anger. He looked at the stubborn expressions on the faces of the O'Malleys. "Very well, build your own boat!"

At two different places in the fire-lit space both groups began the preparations to build their boats.

The gallowglasses and kerns under Dermot

of Dursey felled tall young trees which could be split into planks. Others were set to look for supple osiers. Trees, thirty feet long, were dragged into the enclosure and split. Then with fast strokes of the axe they were smoothed and shaped and set in piles. Meanwhile the horsehides had been scraped clear of rough fat and trimmed.

People sat about the fires late into that night. Their strength had returned. If they could cross the Shannon, then they had a good chance of survival.

The O'Malleys sat by themselves and spoke in conspiratorial voices. Soon they would be in Connacht where they would abandon O'Sullivan Beare and march west to Mayo. They were tired of the battles and the wars.

O'Sullivan Beare came to visit Fiach's and Emar's mother. He sat beside her and looked at her exhausted face. He remembered her as the most delightful and refined of women who had graced his castle with her presence. He recalled her running laughter, the bright flash of humour on her face.

"I brought something for you, my lady," O'Sullivan said.

"Donal Cam brings me a gift during the cold winter. He was always a gallant man," she said weakly.

"And you were a lady born for better things. You should not have followed me on this foolish march."

"But where could I and my children turn?"

"You should have gone to Spain. You would have been welcomed there."

"Then, Donal Cam, make sure my children reach Spain and begin a new life there. I know I shall not make the crossing of the dark waters," she said weakly.

"Then drink this noble wine. It is the last bottle." O'Sullivan Beare held the delicate wine to her lips and she sipped it.

"It is like honey, Donal Cam, and not to be taken with horse meat," she said with humour.

"Certainly not to be taken with horse meat," he laughed. "Now sleep. We will rest here for another day."

She lay back and fell into a deep sleep. The wine had reminded her of Spain. She recalled the fair ship with the crowded sails which had carried her south. The soft evening wind was blowing through the streets and cooling the courtyards and the rooms beyond the balconies. Somewhere a gypsy was playing a guitar and there was the firm tap of dancing feet. She was drinking spiced wine and then she was falling sleep.

When Emar stirred her shoulder the following morning and she did not move she knew that her mother was dead. She felt her forehead. It was as cold as ice. Emar rushed to her brother.

"Mother is dead," she cried. "She died during the night."

Fiach knelt beside his mother and began to pray for the repose of her soul.

"I will prepare a grave for her," Hugh said.

Fiach rose. "No! I will dig it myself. I wish to mark it so that someday when there is peace I will return and raise a monument above my mother."

Fiach went into the woods and in an open spot close to a small stream he began to dig the grave. The earth was iron-hard and he broke the surface with difficulty. Then, while tears poured down his face he shovelled up the undersoil. He recalled the pleasant life they had once lived at their father's castle and the rough fortune which had since befallen them. His mother should never have undertaken the march. She had been born for better things.

Fiach returned to the camp. Already the work of building the boats was in progress. Two rows of osiers had been trimmed and were now set in the ground. The ends were bent to meet each other and the men were binding them with leather thongs. The great boat was taking shape.

Fiach passed down to where some women sat about the pallet of wood fashioned by Hugh. His mother had been stitched into a rough shroud. At a signal, four women lifted the pallet and they moved through the activities of the camp towards the stream. Here the mother was laid to rest beside a winter stream, far from the voices of the sea which she loved so well. Fiach set the earth about her body in a gentle manner. His sister remained while he finished the burial. They stood above the dark mound in silence for some minutes.

"We must leave now. We cannot linger here. There is much preparation to be made."

"Will we survive this journey?" Emar asked, as they returned to the enclosure.

"We must," Fiach answered.

When they returned to the camp they found that the large boat supervised by

Dermot of Dursey was taking firm shape over the framework of osiers. Men were now fixing planks to the skeletal outline and securing them with thongs. Towards evening the horse-hides were secured to the timber frame and the boat could be turned upright. It was twenty-six feet long, six feet wide, and five feet deep.

"Will it float?" askcd one of the kerns.

Dermot of Dursey looked at him in anger. "Do you think that I began without knowing, you bodach! I did not have twelve horses slaughtered to build some useless toy. But it needs seats and cross beams to hold it together and oars have to be shaped. Our work is not yet finished."

In the meantime the O'Malleys were building their own craft. It was in the form of a great barrel, the base secured by horse hide.

"It is without method or shape," Dermot of Dursey commented when he saw the ugly coracle. He suppressed a smile, knowing how quickly the O'Malleys would take offence.

They waited for the night and the thin light of the quarter moon.

"Move forward!" Dermot of Dursey ordered

when he was satisfied that it was sufficiently dark. They moved along the path they had cut out during the day. Fifty men carried the hide-bound boat between them. The O'Malleys followed behind with their light coracle and behind them again followed some of the giollas with pack animals.

They reached the dark swirling waters and slid the boat out into the river. She floated easily. Thirty men with their arms went aboard. Dermot of Dursey had picked the finest oarsmen to make the first crossing. Two horses were secured but if they panicked the men were ordered to cut the ropes.

"Oars at the ready!" Dermot of Dursey ordered. The boat was pushed out into the river. The horses were driven forward and they plunged into the sullen waters, neighing in fear.

"Now. Dip your oars," Dermot called and at his order the men began to row, one of them calling out the beat. The men held their breaths. The boat was performing properly; the timbers held and the hides kept it watertight. The only sound was the plash of oars and the monotonous voice of the man calling out the strokes. They reached the far side of the river and found a landing place.

Carefully they disembarked on the Connacht side of the Shannon.

The O'Malleys, not to be outdone, launched their coracle as soon as Dermot of Dursey returned across the river. Ten of them boarded the curious craft and ordered their followers to give them a final push. They started paddling furiously. But they had not calculated on the swiftness of the current and somewhere on its way across the river the coracle overturned. The O' Malleys called out in the darkness. Then there was silence.

"Let the next thirty men embark," Dermot of Dursey ordered. "It was folly to build such a frail craft but they would not listen."

In Redwood Castle, Donnchadh MacEgan considered his position. Perhaps he should have permitted O'Sullivan's army to cross the Shannon. In trying to prove his allegiance to the Queen, MacEgan was now faced with a beleaguered enemy. Driven by hunger they would surely attack his castle. It was weakly defended and could be easily taken by a trained army.

"What are they doing in the woods?" MacEgan asked one of his followers as he peered down from the battlements. He watched the smoke move lazily skywards; he listened to the trees being felled; he could even smell the aroma of cooking meat.

Fear began to eat into MacEgan's mind as he came to the castle battlements several times during the day and looked down into the woods. It was only in the early dawn that he realised what had happened. He could not believe his eyes as he watched the soldiers disembark on the far side of the river. He noted that the baggage had yet to be ferried across and made a quick decision. His soldiers were wakened and ordered to prepare for action.

With the coming of morning most of the soldiers had been ferried across the river. It now remained for Dermot of Dursey to ferry over the woman, the sutlers, and the baggage which lay stacked beside the river bank. All were guarded by forty men under the command of Thomas Burke who lay in waiting some distance from the river bank, their muskets ready.

And then Donnchadh MacEgan appeared at the edge of the wood leading his soldiers forward, his sword drawn. The women and the sutlers began to scream in terror as

MacEgan's men hacked furiously at them. Fiach, not knowing what to do, grabbed his sister by the hand and ran towards the river.

"I cannot swim," she cried.

"Our only safety lies in the river," he shouted and began to swim. He carried his sister with him.

Meanwhile Thomas Burke and his men emerged from the woods. A quick battle followed in which Donnchadh MacEgan was hacked to death and fifteen of his followers slain.

Wet and tired, Fiach drew his sister ashore. They looked back to the woods where their mother now lay at peace and then they turned and looked towards Connacht. They wondered what lay ahead.

12
In Connacht

he boat made its final crossing, carrying Thomas Burke and his men. Dermot of Dursey was the last to come ashore.

"What shall we do with the boat Donal?" he asked O'Sullivan Beare.

"We will use the hides for footwear. Break up the boat. It has served us well."

Quickly the hides were torn from the boat and cut. The timbers were severed from the osier frame and, plank by plank, thrown into the river. O'Sullivan's followers watched the white planks move slowly out into the river, then hurry downstream, caught by the rushing current.

O'Sullivan Beare drew up his forces on the flat rushy land. The sight of duck passing across the sky in black formation seemed to add to the desolation of the place. Silver birch and sally bushes broke the monotony of the horizon. The deep frost held the marshy place firm beneath their bodies.

As O'Sullivan surveyed his troops he realised the toll taken of them during the past days. Eighty men formed the advance guard and two hundred defended the rear. Between them was wedged the baggage, the sutlers and the camp followers.

O'Sullivan ordered the march to begin and they moved forward across the bleak plain. They had gathered strength from their rest in Redwood Castle forest but they did not waste their energy in talk. Their minds were on the second half of the journey across Connacht.

The spy had lain amongst the river rushes in his light boat, posted there by Tadhg O'Madden who had received news that O'Sullivan Beare and his army were cornered between the Brosna and the Shannon rivers and were about to build a large boat to cross the Shannon.

"Is it possible that they could build a boat to carry so many across?" Tadhg O'Madden had asked.

"They are seafarers, that I know. But little else I picked up save that MacEgan is in his castle and refuses to move against them."

"He will move if he sees a weakness," Tadhg remarked, knowing the character of an old enemy. "But we must keep watch. Go and remain alert."

So the spy listened during the night and watched during the day. He carried with him oaten bread and some beer and he was wrapped in a large mantle. He drew a cover over his boat and was well protected from the cold. When the final boat load of O'Sullivan's followers moved across the waters, he left his light craft and passed through the reeds to the dún of O'Madden.

"Soon they will march through our territory. I heard talk of gold but I am not sure if they carry it or not."

"They are bound to carry gold. We will attack them on the flanks but we will not engage them in battle," said O'Madden.

They prepared for an attack, slipped out of the dún in groups of ten and waited for the advancing enemy.

O'Sullivan Beare's army was only half a mile from the Shannon bank when the first flight

of spears passed into the baggage animals,
setting up a panic amongst them. The sutlers
and women dragged at the manes of the
animals to settle them.

"Keep marching. Keep marching!" Hugh
called. Several of the pack animals were
abandoned along with some followers who
were wounded. The army pushed on . Behind
them they could hear the neighing of animals
as they were slaughtered by the O'Maddens
who also stole the baggage. O'Sullivan's
musketeers had primed their weapons and on
the next attack, they sent withering fire
among the enemy.

The O'Maddens followed O'Sullivan for
some distance but then gave up the pursuit.

By now the marchers had not slept for
forty-eight hours and they were growing
hungry again. A scouting party returned to
announce that they had discovered a
settlement. The inhabitants had fled at their
approach, leaving food.

"The news could not come at a better time,"
Hugh told Fiach. "I have felt hungry all day."

They turned in the direction of the village
which had been abandoned. It was obvious
that it had been quickly evacuated; fires still
burned in the hearths. O'Sullivan's followers

sat down on the hard earth and rested their weary bodies. The food was divided and men and women chewed on the wheat and the barley as if it was sirloin. The beer warmed the stomachs of the gallowglasses and kerns.

"We will find a wood and shelter there for the night. It will give us time to recover our energies. Half the journey is over. Every day we move forward brings the end nearer," O'Sullivan Beare encouraged his remaining followers.

With reluctance they shook from themselves the lethargy which had settled upon them. They limbered their stiff bodies, fell into position and moved forward.

In the gloom the Black Knight again appeared, dressed in armour and helmeted, on his dark horse. He watched the marchers from the crest of a low hill. Then a mist seemed to swirl about him and he melted into the shadowy evening.

"He brings pestilence and death," the women said to each other. "He is evil and in league with the spirits of darkness."

A murmur of fear passed through the column. Even the soldiers seemed scared.

"He is in league with no devil," Hugh called

to them. "He is an old enemy who wishes to do battle with me. There is no reason to fear him. He is mortal like you and me." The voice of Hugh quietened their fear.

Finally they reached the woods of Killimor where, as soon as they found an open space, the soldiers cut some young trees and secured the place against attack. They lit fires and pitched their tents. It was warm and protected in the enclosure though a sad wind complained among the bare branches.

Hugh came to where Emar and Fiach had pitched their tent and sat beside the fire. From his jerkin he produced an oaten cake. "This is for you princess," he said, smiling and handing her the bread.

"Are you not hungry, Hugh?" she asked.

"No. I have eaten well today. I carried some meat with me which I ate during the march. Have you had time to be sad?" he asked her.

"I wept as we crossed the Shannon but during the march I thought only of the journey ahead."

"We have to cross a wide plain, pass over mountains and then we are at our journey's end," said Hugh.

"And what shall you do at journey's end

Hugh?" Emar asked.

"I shall not reach journey's end, princess. I have been haunted by the Black Knight in my dreams. He will not rest until we engage in single combat."

"But you do not have to fight him, Hugh."

"I must. It is my calling. I am a soldier. I was given a sword when I was twelve. I have lived by the sword ever since."

"We thought that you would remain with us when all this is over," said Emar. "Perhaps you could settle down and till the land."

"No," said Hugh. "I could never settle down. I am a mercenary and I sell my sword to the highest bidder. But you must go to Spain where you will live a noble life. There is no place for you in Ireland. The old families and the old ways are passing. The wars will continue for a while in the north. Then the old order will be defeated. You must go to Spain and begin a new life."

He noticed Emar's feet were bleeding and the flesh had been torn away. "How far have you marched on those feet?" Hugh asked.

"A day."

"And you did not complain?"

"There was no reason to complain. Others are in worse condition," Emar answered.

Hugh put her feet on his lap and began to clean away the dirt from the raw flesh. Then from his purse he drew dried herbs and moss. He placed them on the soles of her feet and bound them with strips of linen. Emar was surprised at how gentle his hands were.

"The herbs will help to scab the feet and the moss will protect them from pain. Now let me make you proper shoes."

Hugh took out his dagger and, placing leather on a log, began to cut it into shape. Quickly he fashioned rough shoes, sewed them together with thongs and drew them over Emar's feet.

"They should see you to the end of the journey. Now I must go and sleep. I have to keep the second watch before dawn." And with that he left them.

"He is so cruel and so gentle," Emar said to her brother. "Do you believe him when he says he will do battle with the Black Knight?"

"Yes. They will fight."

"And will Hugh die?"

Fiach did not answer her question.

They looked into the heart of the fire and thought of the lonely grave in which their mother lay on the far side of the Shannon. Life was empty without her and the future uncertain.

"It is time to sleep," Fiach said.

His sister lay in the tent and soon fell fast asleep. Fiach, lying on his back and wrapped in his great mantle, looked at the mysterious stars pulsing brilliantly above him. He gazed at them for some time. Then he too fell asleep.

13
Victory at Aughrim

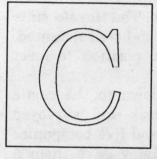aptain Henry Malby
listened to his scouts
give details of the army
and followers of O'Sullivan Beare.

"Three hundred soldiers you say?"

"Fewer and they are battle weary. A fresh
well-trained army would wipe them out. They
have no taste for further action," one of the
messengers told Malby.

Malby could muster five or six hundred
men. He would pick his own battle ground.
On sloping terrain a cavalry charge would
break the resistance of the weary gallowglasses. The battle would be at Aughrim.

As Malby sat considering the plan of battle
he heard the sound of horses passing through
the great gate. He went to the window and
looked down into the courtyard. The Earl of

Clanricarde's brother had arrived with fresh troops. Malby invited him to his room to drink some wine and quickly told him of the approaching army.

"Hardly an army," Clanricarde's brother replied, "more like a rabble. The terrain suits us and our men are fresh and well mounted. Let us move forward into position to meet them."

The two men walked down to the castle yard, mounted their horses and surveyed their two troops of horse and five companies of foot. Captain Henry Malby gave them a brief description of the army they were about to encounter. He promised them spoils when victory was secured. At a signal they moved confidently forward.

Within an hour they were in position. They stood concealed in a wood and waited for O'Sullivan Beare. The trap had been set.

That morning Fiach joined Hugh at the rear of the army where it was felt that they would be attacked. They marched twelve miles northwards from Killimor wood looking for some sign of a village where they could obtain food. But there was none.

Then the enemy appeared on the hill of

Aughrim. An army in full formation advanced from the woods led by two captains; behind the mounted troops came the companies of footsoldiers.

It was too much for those in the van of O'Sullivan's army. Panicking, they broke formation and fled for cover leaving the baggage train exposed.

Hugh rushed forward and saw the fresh troops ready to engage in battle. This was the first army O'Sullivan's men encountered in battle formation. The odds were against them. They would be slaughtered.

At this point O'Sullivan Beare proved himself a leader of men. He stood a little away from his troops and followers and addressed them in a firm voice.

"Who would not rather fall fighting in battle, avenging your blood, than like cattle, perish in cowardly flight. There is none to come to our aid. The enemy blocks the roads and passes. We are wearied with our long journey and unable to run. Fear not a worthless mob who are not used to fighting as we are."

O'Sullivan had no sooner finished when the enemy cavalry charged at full tilt, trying to run his soldiers through with their spears.

The charge was beaten back.

O'Sullivan Beare quickly called out the battle orders and immediately his soldiers fell into position. They knew precisely what was expected of them.

"We must find an advantage," O'Sullivan called to them. He pointed to a narrow way between a bog and swampy ground, where Malby's cavalry, now certain of victory, dismounted and with the pikemen advanced through the narrow place.

Several of O'Sullivan's musketeers took up position and discharged shot into the enemy lines which threw them into confusion. Then the kerns and gallowglasses turned and charged, bringing their great axes down upon the heads of the enemy cavalry officers. Madness seemed to possess their minds and bodies .

The enemy suffered heavy losses in the narrow place. Some rushed across the bog, others were trampled upon. Eventually Malby's men regrouped and for a time they held their ground.

"Kill the leaders!" Hugh roared to his men. "It will break the spirit of the enemy."

Maurice O'Sullivan closed with Richard Burke but was struck on the chest and knocked down. His coat of mail saved him from death. Then Richard Burke's arm was hacked off by one of O'Sullivan's men. Maurice jumped to his feet and and ran Richard Burke through with his pike. Nor did Malby survive the battle. He was quickly dismissed by two swordsmen. The enemy, seeing that their leaders had been killed, fled the battle field in confusion. What seemed certain defeat for O'Sullivan had been turned to victory. A great cheer went up from the camp followers.

Hugh wished to pursue the enemy.

"We have no time to lose," O'Sullivan Beare told him. "We must press forward. We cannot rest. Gather the enemy's arms and colours and let us advance."

O'Sullivan left behind fourteen dead. The enemy had lost a hundred men.

Fiach left the vanguard and returned to where the camp followers and the sutlers were trying desperately to keep the order of march. The battle had thrown them into confusion and panic was beginning to spread through the ranks. But they knew from the expression on O'Sullivan Beare's face that he was determined to move as far north as he could.

"But must we march at this pace?" Emar argued with her brother.

"If we rest the enemy will regroup. We cannot afford another battle so we cannot afford to stop," he answered.

"And what of those who who can no longer endure the pace. What will happen to them?"

He did not answer. Emar stopped talking and concentrated on the march. She had to force herself to move forward despite bitter cold and utter fatigue. She tried to stifle all though and feeling. She looked at those marching ahead of her. They were being pushed beyond endurance. Some limped forward, their feet torn by the hard ground. Families tried to keep together, throwing their arms about each other for comfort and security. But now and then someone fell away from the line and collapsed upon the frozen earth. The others did not bother to turn about but continued to struggle forward.

Hugh noticed that for the first time the soldiers were beginning to suffer from fatigue. They had marched impossible distances, fought continual skirmishes, defended the camps at night-time and endured the deep frosts. Their limbs were weary. The sharpness had gone from their eyes. They had lost the taste for battle. Towards the horizon Hugh saw that sinister figures followed at a distance, living in the shadows, waiting for someone to fall by the wayside. When the musketeers fired at them, they retreated to a safe distance, then reappeared again.

The day passed into evening and his followers cried out that there should be a short stop but O'Sullivan Beare handed down the order that they must march through the night. And as the evening deepened the snow began to fall. It had fallen already on the higher ground and as they passed up out of the plain they encountered heavy drifts. The sutlers cursed the few remaining horses and pulled them forwards. The pace of the march slowed down to a crawl. People held onto each other in the dark as they moved forward through the night. The cold became intense. It cut through clothes and flesh and entered the bone.

"I cannot continue," Emar said.

Fiach put her arm about his shoulder and dragged her forward through the snow. From somewhere within him he seemed to discover a hidden strength. He called out to her that she must not give up.

They passed on, moving up towards the summit of Saint Mary. The snow grew deeper and now they struggled forward, almost incapable of lifting their feet. Many gave up the struggle and quietly waited to die.

"It was a foolish move," said Hugh. We should have rested in the lowlands. We could have regained some of our strength. Instead we have lost half our soldiers and we stand little chance against our enemies. And the Burkes deserted us for Mayo during the night." He spoke to Fiach and Emar as they stood on the summit of Saint Mary's and surveyed the vast scene which stretched before them, a white landscape full of enemies and obstacles.

The struggling group now moved downhill, again falling into their old formation. They had seen a castle in the distance and O'Sullivan Beare decided upon a ruse to obtain food.

"Let us march forward with the royal standards captured at Aughrim. We may received hospitality from friends of the Queen." They marched towards the castle.

MacDavitt, the owner of the castle, stood at the battlements. There was a smile upon his face as he watched the army move down the road towards him, carrying the royal standards. He might have been deceived by the ruse but already he had received news from Aughrim. A horseman had ridden all day with the message that O'Sullivan Beare lived off the countryside. MacDavitt had ordered all the villages to hide their food and drink and drive the herds away from the line of march.

"I come in the name of her majesty and I carry her majesty's standards," cried O'Sullivan Beare.

"And have you been to Aughrim?" MacDavitt asked.

"Aye, and a glorious battle it was. We defeated the rebels who had marched into the territory."

"And what do you seek here?"

"Food and shelter."

"Then you may have food and shelter. Stones to eat and spears to cover you." And with that missiles poured from the ramparts of the castle. O'Sullivan Beare and his men beat a hasty retreat, humiliated.

As the march continued the snow grew deep and wet and the marchers had to drag their way wearily through it with no time to take a rest. It was a long savage day. The spirit of the army had been broken and soldiers now became little better than stragglers, moving blindly towards Leitrim and, perhaps, hospitality at the castle of O'Rourke. Men were too tired to curse O'Sullivan Beare who plodded ahead like the others. But one figure gave them courage and that was Dermot of Dursey. Despite his age and the great festering gashes in his feet he dragged himself forward.

"Have people no mercy or Christian spirit? They must see that we starve and are in need of rest," Emar pleaded.

"Expect no help from them. They will attack us, given the chance. They know that we carry a chest of gold," Hugh told her.

"I can move no further, Hugh. I wish to die here." With that she moved out of the straggling crowd, fell and was almost buried by the soft snow.

"You cannot give up now. The end is in sight. Another day or two and we will be in the north. Then we will find hospitality." He took her body in his arms, lifted her frail figure on his shoulder and continued to march forward.

Fiach was coming to the end of his strength. He had watched strong men collapse and die. To escape the horror about him he recalled warm evenings in their castle in Kerry when the logs were drawn into the great hall and placed upon the fire. How he wished that the wars had not taken place, that the great families had not been broken, that the lands had not passed out of the Irish chieftains' hands.

He looked at the stragglers ahead of him and recalled the strong army which had set out some ten days ago. They had not known then that they were marching towards their deaths. Had they remained in Kerry they might have survived.

"It is a brave and a foolish march," Fiach said to Hugh.

"It started out bravely. Now it has become a rout. One more battle and we are destroyed." Hugh was beginning to doubt the wisdom of the whole venture. Even his great body was weary after the tribulations of the journey.

All that day O'Sullivan and his followers pushed ahead through the rough and cheerless lands of Roscommon, the

MacDavitts following them at a distance and harrying them whenever they got a chance.

Hugh sighted Sliabh O'Flynn. There were woods where they could hide from the enemy and rest their weary limbs. They reached the woods and found a place to camp.

They had scarcely settled down when a man advanced through the trees. He had a noble bearing and he came directly to O'Sullivan Beare. "If the MacDavitts knew I was here they would slay both me and my family. At this moment they are coming through the woods. They intend to slaughter you in your sleep," said the man.

"Thank you stranger. You are the first one to take pity on our plight, the first friend we have encountered in a long journey. Here, take this for you and your family." O'Sullivan handed him a small purse of Spanish gold and the stranger slipped into the woods.

O'Sullivan Beare considered his position for a moment. "We cannot rest here. Let us move on further," he ordered.

"No. Let us rest. We have been pushed beyond endurance," said a follower.

O'Sullivan said harshly. "I am moving forward. If you wish to follow you may. If you wish to remain here, then that is your choice."

O'Sullivan moved up through the mountains and instinctively they followed him. He stopped only once and that was to set large fires blazing. "Our enemies will think that we are camping in the woods. It will give us a chance to move ahead of them," he said.

Quickly the fires were built by the weary soldiers. They were set alight and the crackling flames shot heavenwards. The fires had a hypnotic effect and the marchers looked at them with desire in their eyes. But the order was given to move on.

They passed up into almost impenetrable forest tangled with undergrowth and brambles and they had to force their way through, hacking a pathway. The wind from the north set up a high-pitched wail. The marchers blundered forward trying to follow the voice of Hugh. Finally they reached open ground again.

As dawn approached the MacDavitts discovered they had been deceived. They found the tracks left by the retreating marchers and followed them until they finally came upon the exhausted soldiers of O'Sullivan Beare.

O'Sullivan prepared to meet them. "We

will fight them rather than quit this spot. Let us die facing them rather than have them plunge their spears in our backs," he cried. Sixty soldiers fell into formation and advanced upon the MacDavitts. Courage surged through their bodies and they fought with vigour. Surprised by the onslaught, the enemy turned and fled, melting into the woods.

O'Sullivan Beare ordered two horses to be slaughtered and started several fires. Soon the horse flesh was roasting on spits and giving off a strong aroma. The hungry men chewed upon the flesh, the blood and juice running from their mouths on to their tunics. Even Emar ate the rough meat. Her body was exhausted and Fiach had to cut the flesh into fine slivers to feed his sister. Her face was thin and gaunt, dark circles ringed her eyes and her fragile skin was chapped by the cold.

Fiach cursed O'Sullivan Beare. "I should not have followed him," he said to one of the soldiers.

"He has learned a hard lesson," the soldier replied. "He has learned that the old cause for which he fought is dead. Those who might have protected him have become his enemies. The Queen now rules Ireland."

"And so the march was futile," groaned Fiach.

"Yes. It only remains for us to return to our homes. Already the O'Malleys have left. Others will follow in their footsteps. There is nothing left to fight for. Even O'Sullivan's gold will not buy food during this winter."

Fiach could see that discontent was rife among the soldiers. After the meal they sought shelter beneath the trees, threw themselves down on the ground and soon they were asleep. They had marched fifty miles and they had fought a battle. Their strength and courage had been tested to the limit.

Fiach discovered a protected place for his sister, a ledge of rock and beneath it a pile of leaves. She lay in the comfort of the sheltered place and fell asleep. Fiach slept close by, sword at the ready.

14
The Duel

As morning light broke in the wood Fiach shook his sister awake. She had slept soundly and had recovered some of her strength. He took some charred meat from his satchel and, again cutting it finely, forced her to eat it.

"This is a most comfortable shelter," she said, feeling the soft moss. "I wish that I could remain here."

"A day's journey and we will reach the safety of O'Rourke's castle. Only two women remain after the long journey. All the rest have perished," he told her.

"And our mother lies in the woods far away beside the lonely Shannon."

"Yes. Some day I will return to her grave and place a noble stone above it. But now we must make ready to move."

O'Sullivan's followers now passed through bog and marsh covered in deep snow. On the flanks of small hills stood wintery woods, black and mysterious. Here and there a dark stream, in troubled voice, passed quickly down the slope towards a river. They waded through the freezing waters almost unconscious of the cold. They saw smoke rising from a cabin but nowhere could they see man or beast. They moved through a white desert.

And then ahead of them appeared the Black Knight, dressed in his dark armour and moving towards them, followed by Peccata his dwarf. As the Black Knight drew near they could hear the jangle of his spurs. They looked at the mysterious figure and wondered if he was death coming upon a fatal visit.

"Hugh the Gallowglass, we have a fight to finish," the knight called, raising his lance.

"Do not heed him, Hugh," Fiach pleaded. "Deafen your ears to his challenge. He has waited until you are weak."

"And so you have travelled this great distance to do battle with a simple soldier," Hugh called to the Black Knight.

"No simple soldier but the strongest born and an enemy to me. Prepare for battle!"

"I am weary with travel. You have been sustained by food."

"Prepare for battle!" the Black Knight called.

"Do not listen to him, Hugh. He is evil," Fiach pleaded.

"I know he has a black soul," said Hugh. He took his great sword from his scabbard and held it in his hands. "I go to battle, my good friend Fiach. I shall not see you again. At some quieter time in Spain pray for the soldier Hugh." And with that he moved forward to meet the Black Knight, holding his sword in both hands and keeping a close eye on the cunning enemy. Then the knight urged his horse forward and thundered towards Hugh. There was the clash of sword on armour as they met and Hugh fell to the ground. The knight quickly turned and again charged. His lance pierced the body of the great gallowglass. Hugh remained upright for a moment, drew his dagger and with a final surge of strength threw it at the Black Knight. It caught the knight's throat and he fell from his black horse.

Then there was a running crack of ice, the

snow opened and both the Black Knight and
Hugh were drawn into a mysterious hole.
O'Sullivan's followers look in amazement at
the scene.

"He knew it would happen," Fiach said to
Emar. "He told me often but I did not believe
him."

"I shall always keep him in my prayers,"
said Emar.

Fiach recalled the days he had spent with
Hugh during the long march. A brave and
simple man, he had been born to the practice
of war and had died in combat. Hugh's life
was at an end but Fiach must live on for he
had his sister to care for.

O'Sullivan and his men marched on to a
mysterious wood. It must once have been a
sacred place for a great dolmen stood at the
edge. The trees were dense and so they felt
safe from the attack of an enemy. Exhausted,
they threw themselves upon the ground and
fell asleep. O'Sullivan Beare, with twelve
men, remained awake. They lit fires at the
edge of the wood to direct stragglers who
were following. Then they sat about the
biggest fire and looked into its warm heart.
They had little wish to talk of the past days.

In the town of Boyle, Oliver Lambert, President of Connacht, sat down to supper with his friend John Napier. He felt secure in the Norman town which stood upon a river and was well fortified. He had almost secured the surrounding area for the Queen but to the north lay hostile country which he dared not penetrate.

He ate his food with relish and washed it down with good French wine. He had marched for a whole day and he felt a chill in his bones.

Lambert was anxious to discover where the renegade, O'Sullivan Beare, lay hidden. His information was patchy. He knew that O'Sullivan had engaged in battle at Aughrim and that he had a formidable army. But Lambert's spies had told him that already many of the army were returning to their homes in the north. Two of O'Sullivan's men had been captured and were now on their way to Boyle to be questioned. Lambert was eager for news.

"It certainly would be a feather in my cap to finish off the villain once and for all. Everywhere his cause is in disarray. It is only a matter of time before he will have been killed or forced to flee to Spain," Lambert told his friends. He sucked at a rotten tooth as he talked. The cold had started a nerve and he wished that he could kill the pain.

"And where is O'Sullivan at this present moment?" Lambert's host asked.

"Skulking in some wood or other with no taste for battle anymore. If we could flush him out into the open then we could cut his army to pieces. I am sure that they are exhausted."

It was late in the day when the two deserters were brought to Boyle. When they were taken to the dungeon they were given food which they ate like famished wolves. Their hair was matted and in the confined space there was a raw stench from their bodies. The deserters refused to talk unless they were guaranteed free passage from the town. One of the captains sent a messenger to Lambert seeking directions.

The reply was simple. "Offer them anything they seek. When they have given you the information you require, kill them. They are outlaws."

The two told the captain a most extraordinary story. It sounded so incredible that the captain felt they were lying but they swore that all they related was true.

"It is a most remarkable story," Oliver Lambert remarked, when the captain told him of the long march. "This O'Sullivan is a brave but foolish man, but now he is hungry and and his army begins to abandon him. Make ready to engage him."

"And what shall I do with the informers?" asked the captain.

"Execute them. Place their heads on spikes and let all outlaws know that the Queen's writ now runs in Boyle."

All night the fires burned in the forest and all night the followers of O'Sullivan Beare slept. In the morning people in the locality, who had watched the fires burn during the night, came to investigate. They often came to the woods to cut timber but they were surprised to find the exhausted marchers. O'Sullivan Beare, seeing that they were unarmed, invited them into the camp where he soon discovered that the villagers owed allegiance to the old cause.

The leader of the village spoke: "Some of us once marched south with O'Neill and we know the hard conditions of the route. I will send some of my people to bring you food. In the meantime we will spread the rumour that you are woodcutters gathering fuel. That will throw the spies off your trail. They are everywhere. Even old friends now offer allegiance to the Queen. The defeat at Kinsale has changed everything."

Soon panniers of food were carried to the starving people in the wood. The bread and meat tasted better than any they had eaten before. They ate at their leisure and soon a small hope was kindled in their hearts.

"Perhaps we may reach our goal after all," O'Sullivan remarked to himself. He went to the great chest and taking out several small purses of gold he gave them to those who had brought food.

While they ate, a messenger arrived saying that Lambert had set up blocks on the main routes into Leitrim.

"Then we will have to make a night march across the Curlew mountains to escape the watchful eyes of Lambert's men. We must rest for the day and gather our strength," O'Sullivan ordered.

Close to the warm fires his army rested while the villagers kept watch. The short day passed quickly and, when night began to fall, they rose stiffly and fell into marching order. There now remained sixty people, between soldiers, sutlers and Emar. They said goodbye to the villagers and began the journey into the mountains.

They avoided all marked tracks and passed into the woods. After three hours marching they were lost. They decided to pitch camp in the forest and wait for the morning. They had built a small fire in a hollow when suddenly a stranger appeared from among the trees, a spectral figure dressed in white linen, his face gaunt and his feet bare.

He spoke in a thin whisper. "I have come to guide you. Trust in me. I know of your long journey from the south and I know these mountains better than anyone else alive."

O'Sullivan Beare wondered if the strange creature who now offered to lead them could be mad. He might even be an agent of the enemy and lead them into a trap. But O'Sullivan knew that they were lost and he decided to trust him so they passed through the forest, following the strange guide.

During the night they stopped at a mountain village where they were able to purchase food. After resting they continued their journey. As morning light filled the sky they looked down upon a wide plain.

"My journey ends here and my task is

completed." The spectral figure pointed into the distance. "There lies O'Rourke's castle. You will find hospitality there."

"You have done well. Here, accept this gold." O'Sullivan Beare offered him a purse of Spanish gold.

The stranger accepted the gold, said goodbye and passed up into the forest.

O'Sullivan Beare and the others looked into the distance where they could see the turrets of a castle in the grey light.

Fiach turned towards Emar. "We have survived. To night we will rest in a warm room and eat good food."

She could not speak. Tears ran down her face. She had almost completed the great march against all the terrible odds.

They moved down towards the snow bound plains.

15
Leitrim at Last

I t was the morning of 14 January and the winter sky was luminous with cold light as the weary marchers moved forward towards the distant castle. O'Connor Kerry rode on a stray beast, his feet livid with broken ulcers. The others shuffled along on worn shoes made from the flayed hides of slaughtered horses. The men's beards had not been cut during the journey. Their faces were haggard, their eyes sunken and the flesh had fallen from their bodies. But they still marched at the head of the small group, proud that they had survived so great and dangerous a journey.

In the lead was O'Sullivan Beare, his head high, his eyes haunted. He had led his people across Ireland in the depths of winter and all but a few had perished. The memory of the long march would never leave him.

Trudging in the middle of the column, Emar felt her strength fail. Her body was thin and frail and even the food at the village had not added to her strength. She fell on the hard ground and cut her knees. Fiach lifted her on to her feet.

"Only a few miles more and it will all be over," he whispered. "Feel proud that you are the only woman to survive the march."

"My head reels and turns. Strange visions appear before me. I see my mother again. She is riding across the wide lawn towards the sea shore. The white sails crowd the masts of ships as they leave for Spain. Now I see her pass through the streets of Seville. She is in a courtyard with marble columns. She is young and her face is lit with happiness." Emar began to walk away from the group, her mind disturbed and tangled. Fiach wondered if she were going mad. On the march he had heard some of the old woman chatter oddly to themselves before they fell by the wayside. He took her arm and directed her forward.

Nobody paid any attention to her strange talk. They were interested only in reaching the fort.

"Is it much further?" a sutler called.

"Seven miles," came the reply.

"Then it is seven miles too far," he cried and having spoken the words he fell dead as if his heart had burst. All looked in pity at the body of the servant who was almost within reach of help when his spirit failed.

On the column's flank a horseman broke from a small wood and rode west. One of Lambert's spies had taken careful note of the number of marchers who had survived; there were thirty-five.

Early in the morning Brian O'Rourke caught a glimpse of the straggling band of marchers from the battlements of his castle. He wondered who they could be. He was expecting neither friend nor enemy. The weather had thrown a fortress about his land. Perhaps some village had been attacked by Lambert and the inhabitants were seeking refuge in his kingdom.

"Do they carry standards?" O'Rourke asked one of his men.

"No. But they seem to be the remnants of an army of gallowglasses and kerns."

"Then they must be coming from the south.

The wars run against our friends in Munster."

"Surely not from the south in this weather," a soldier replied. "Shall we go and find out if they are friends or enemies?"

"They are friends. Of that have no doubt. No enemy would dare enter my territory, so ill-prepared."

When they were still a mile from the castle Brian O'Rourke recognised O'Sullivan Beare. "It is Donal Cam. I would recognise him anywhere. But he is far from his lands and surely he can place a better army in the field. He looks tired. Let us go and greet him."

O'Rourke passed down the stone steps of the tower to the courtyard. He gathered his mantle about him and mounted his white horse. His men marched behind, two carrying drums. He ordered the great gate to be opened. It creaked inward on ponderous hinges. He ordered the drummers to beat out a marching step and he moved forward followed by his men.

The straggling marchers heard the drumbeats. Instinctively the soldiers grabbed their swords and prepared for an attack. But as they looked towards the castle they saw

Brian O'Rourke advance with his men, marching firmly to the tuck of the drum.

O'Rourke stopped in front of O'Sullivan Beare and dismounted. Then opening his cloak, he threw his arms about his fellow chieftain. "You have marched a long way Donal Cam. Where are your soldiers?"

"Their bodies mark the bloody path which has led us here. We found no comfort in any castle or at any village save one. We have been harassed by those who now turn to the Queen for protection. The old cause is dead, Brian. The wars are over."

"Come!" said O'Rourke. "You will find food and shelter at my castle. Do you wish to ride my horse?"

"I have marched this far and I will march to the very end. I would like to lead my people through the gateway of your castle."

O'Sullivan's small band set off on the last mile flanked by the army of Brian O'Rourke. The long march was almost over. It was approaching eleven o'clock when they passed into the courtyard. For the first time in fifteen days they were behind protected ramparts.

Soon a great fire blazed in the courtyard. The surviving marchers gathered about the flames, unable to believe that the ordeal was over. Numb with emotion, they looked in disbelief at the great castle. And then many of them began to sob as some deep pain was drawn from them. The occupants of the castle respected their strange sorrow.

Food was carried to O'Sullivan's followers and they ate ravenously. They broke the bread into large chunks and stuffed it into their mouths. They drank the beer as quickly as it was poured. They behaved like half-famished animals.

Emar alone ate daintily. An old woman rubbed honey on her lips which Emar licked with her tongue. Then she opened her mouth and the woman fed her with shallow spoonfuls. Later she took small pieces of food and some wine.

"She is in deep distress," the old woman told Fiach. "Her mind has had to endure more than it can bear."

"I know," Fiach told the old woman. "She has witnessed much hardship and death during the last weeks."

"She has put a lock on her mind," answered the old woman. "It will take many days to find the key to open it. But I will take good care of her. I will bring her to a quiet room where she will sleep deeply."

Fiach sat down before the fire, deep in thought. His body and mind were weary. He wished to have time to rest and think.

In the far corner of the courtyard the great chest had been opened. O'Sullivan Beare stood it on a barrel and set about paying the soldiers who had survived. When he had finished paying them he took another purse from the chest and then ordered it to be closed.

He walked to where Fiach was sitting and sat beside him. It was the first time he had been so familiar since the march began.

"What will you do now?" O'Sullivan asked.

"Our lands have been taken from us. I will follow all the others into exile in Spain and become a soldier of fortune like Hugh."

"You were born for better things. The King of Spain will need secretaries and diplomats. You must finish your schooling and go to the university. Study the humanities and discover the glory of man. I have often wished for the life of study during the past weeks. But I will never get rest while I remain in

Ireland. There are so many battles to be fought. Here, I brought something for you. It is a gift from Hugh. He wished you to have it." And with that O'Sullivan handed Fiach a heavy bag of gold.

"I cannot take it."

"You must. Hugh would be offended if you refused."

Fiach took the heavy purse of gold and placed it about his neck.

"There will be several ships sailing from Donegal to Spain and you will receive protection on the way to the coast," said O'Sullivan.

"I will consider your advice," Fiach said, no longer in awe of the chieftain.

For Fiach the day passed quietly in the castle. Several of the young men asked him to tell of his great exploit but he had no wish to recount it. Instead he walked up the stairs to the battlements and looked out at the Curlew mountains covered in deep snow. It was difficult to believe that he had spent last night marching across them. He was about to descend when he saw Dermot of Dursey. Fiach admired the vigorous old man of seventy who had shown so much courage.

"Well young man. Does it all look like a

dream now?" Dermot asked.

"My feet tell me that it was no dream but a harsh march."

"The greatest march of all!" Dermot said with pride. "When it is written down they will tell of our great courage, of the immense difficulties we overcame, of the lack of charity of those who should have been our friends. But come! Tell me what plans you have for yourself."

"O'Sullivan Beare advises me to go to Spain," said Fiach.

"Good advice! In Spain I shall pine for Ireland. I am old and must eat the bitter bread of exile. But you will enjoy Spain. It is filled with white light. It is a young man's world. Come, the darkness draws on. Let us go down to the great hall. Tonight we feast with our host. I look forward to warm food and rich wine. It has been well earned." Dermot laughed as they passed down the narrow stairs.

Fiach went to a room set aside for him. It was a narrow place with a vaulted ceiling. For the first time since he began the march, he had privacy. He washed away the filth and the sweat of the journey. Then he put on a silk shirt. It was soft and gentle to his body.

When Fiach was finished dressing he made his way to the great hall. It was a high spacious place. In the stone fireplace surmounted by the arms of O'Rourke upon a wide lintel, seasoned oak logs were burning. The rich scent filled the hall. Brian O'Rourke stood with the others before the great fire. He greeted Fiach when he entered the hall.

"I have heard of the great courage of both you and your sister. Noble blood runs in your veins and you have not dishonoured your line. You bear a great name which stretches back to the dawn of remembrance. Tonight the genealogies will be sung for us."

O'Rourke clapped his hands and ordered the feast to begin. Immediately the sutlers, the soldiers and the gentlemen made their way to the massive tables set out in a T-shape beneath the great arched roof. They all knew their places in the Gaelic order of things.

Then the finest of meat was set before them. As Fiach cut a slice of beef he remembered the hunger of the long march. But he placed the dark memory behind him. Fine wines from Spain were carried to the table and soon both sutler and lord were in a merry mood. The arched roof echoed to the voice of Dermot of Dursey recounting how the great boat was constructed in the trees beneath Redwood castle.

Course after course of fine food was placed on the tables. When the goblets of wine were emptied a servant was at hand to replenish them. The feast lasted late into the night. Then, when the final course had been eaten, O'Rourke ordered his harper to entertain the company. The musician sat on a dais and when silence descended on the hall he began to play. His music was subtle and quiet, full of strange mystery. It could sooth the mind with its power. It belonged to the old Gaelic world which was passing away. They listened, enraptured, to the gentle music. When it was finished, Dermot of Dursey stepped forward and called out the genealogies of Fiach's family. The ceremony belonged to an heroic age. Fiach listened enthralled as the names of his ancestors were intoned. He knew that he was listening to something which would never happen again. And when it was all over there was an air of sadness in the hall.

"It is time to sleep," O'Rourke called out.

They left the hall and made their way to their rooms to rest.

A week later Emar had recovered from her illness. Her body was still frail but her strength returned a little every day. She had no wish to speak of the terrible journey. She recalled only the summer days at their castle when her mother was alive and the world in which they lived was secure. Fiach knew that he must take her to Spain. There alone she would be happy, in a warm place.

They left the castle a month later, when spring was in the air and the days were lengthening. They rode to Donegal bay under heavy escort. There they boarded a ship bound for Spain.

As the wind caught the white sails Emar and Fiach looked at the coast of Ireland with its high mountains and rugged beauty. They stood watching until it passed beneath the horizon.

Envoi

All during the story the King of Spain had listened intently. Sometimes he asked questions and consulted the map but most of the time he sat thoughtfully on his throne. He was greatly impressed, by the time Fiach drew the story to an end.

"I have followed you both every step of your journey. I have never heard a story quite like it. It must be written down and remembered," said the King.

"We are honoured to be in your presence, Your Majesty. We have been kindly treated ever since our arrival in Spain," said Emar.

"And that is as it should be. We treat the Irish as our own. Now what do you intend to do with your lives? You are young and you must have some dreams."

"At present I am preparing to go to university. And every day my sister receives private tuition," said Fiach.

"It is important that young women should be educated. Have you any particular interest?" the King asked Emar.

"I am learning to read Greek and Latin, your majesty."

"Then you must visit the Escorial library when you have mastered both languages. I believe that we have thousands of manuscripts here. So my librarian tells me. I do not have much time to read. And you Fiach, when you have finished at the university, I wish you to come here as one of my private secretaries. It is interesting work and you can help your country better here than on the battlefield."

"Thank you very much, your majesty," said Fiach.

"Before you leave I have some gifts for you." The King rang a bell and a secretary entered.

"Are the papers and the seals in order?" the King asked.

"Yes your majesty."

"Good. If the young lady will advance

towards my throne I will present her with a gift."

Emar approached the King of Spain. From a velvet box he took a diamond tiara and placed it upon her head.

"You are now a titled lady of Spain. You will receive a pension and, on your marriage, a dowry from the royal treasury."

She bowed towards the King and moved away a little.

Fiach advanced.

"Fiach, I confer upon you the title of Knight of Spain, which you may use when you are twenty-one. You will also receive a royal pension of fifty ducats a month."

The secretary presented the King with an ornamented scroll and with a quick flourish of a quill he inscribed his name upon the paper. Then the secretary, with slow ceremony, placed the King's seal on red wax.

The audience was at an end. Fiach and Emar passed out of the King's chamber and out of the antechamber and into the bright light of Spain.

Before them lay the future.